"May I ki... times' sak...

Logan had never asked to kiss her before. Never had to. They'd been drawn together with the force of an attraction that was far too great to resist.

Jessica knew she should say no. But something inside her wanted to see if she was up to the challenge. To see if she was really over him. The way she told herself she was. The way she wanted to believe. "All right, but no hands."

The moment his lips touched hers, Jessica knew she should have added "no lips" to her clause.

She wasn't over him. If anything, this kiss, so tenderly executed, made it even worse by reminding her how much she missed him.

Jessica was stumbling, heading straight for the abyss that was gaping in front of her. How could she have said yes?

But how could she have said no?

Dear Reader,

Once again, we're back to offer you six fabulous romantic novels, the kind of book you'll just long to curl up with on a warm spring day. Leading off the month is award-winner Marie Ferrarella, whose *This Heart for Hire* is a reunion romance filled with the sharply drawn characters and witty banter you've come to expect from this talented writer.

Then check out Margaret Watson's *The Fugitive Bride,* the latest installment in her CAMERON, UTAH, miniseries. This FBI agent hero is about to learn all about love at the hands of his prime suspect. *Midnight Cinderella* is Eileen Wilks' second book for the line, and it's our WAY OUT WEST title. After all, there's just nothing like a cowboy! Our FAMILIES ARE FOREVER flash graces Kayla Daniels' *The Daddy Trap,* about a resolutely single hero faced with fatherhood—and love. *The Cop and Calamity Jane* is a suspenseful romp from the pen of talented Elane Osborn; you'll be laughing out loud as you read this one. Finally, welcome Linda Winstead Jones to the line. Already known for her historical romances, this author is about to make a name for herself in contemporary circles with *Bridger's Last Stand.*

Don't miss a single one—and then rejoin us next month, when we bring you six more examples of the best romantic writing around.

Yours,

Leslie J. Wainger
Executive Senior Editor

Please address questions and book requests to:
Silhouette Reader Service
U.S.: 3010 Walden Ave., P.O. Box 1325, Buffalo, NY 14269
Canadian: P.O. Box 609, Fort Erie, Ont. L2A 5X3

MARIE FERRARELLA

THIS HEART FOR HIRE

Published by Silhouette Books

America's Publisher of Contemporary Romance

To Leslie Wainger,
for being patient and for being indulgent,
and to my Jessica, for being.

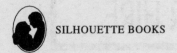 SILHOUETTE BOOKS

ISBN 0-373-07919-2

THIS HEART FOR HIRE

Copyright © 1999 by Marie Rydzynski-Ferrarella

This edition published by arrangement with Harlequin Books S.A.

® and TM are trademarks of Harlequin Books S.A., used under license.
Trademarks indicated with ® are registered in the United States Patent
and Trademark Office, the Canadian Trade Marks Office and in other
countries.

Printed in U.S.A.

MARIE FERRARELLA
lives in southern California. She describes herself as the
tired mother of two overenergetic children and the con-
tented wife of one wonderful man. This RITA Award-
winning author is thrilled to be following her dream of
writing full-time.

Prologue

Maybe the death threats were getting to him.

Logan Buchanan ran a restless hand through his dark blond hair as he stood by the racetrack, watching the mechanic fix his car. Dampness hung in the air like an oppressive blanket, reflecting his mood.

Maybe he was actually beginning to believe the melodramatic threats in the letters he'd been receiving these past few weeks at his home and office. Maybe that was why he felt as if he couldn't find a place for himself lately.

Ironic, wasn't it? Here he was, Logan Buchanan, one of the country's richest men, courtesy of his far-seeing grandfather, able to wallow in any indulgence, satisfy any whim, and yet he felt edgy. Not nervous, edgy. As if nothing was quite right anymore.

Maybe it was more than the threats, he thought.

Maybe the threats had just brought it all home to him. If by some quirk of fate these threats were actually on the level and he died tomorrow, would he really have lived at all? By his own standards, not other people's. Had he really been alive at all by his own standards?

He hadn't felt alive, really alive now for two years. Not since Jessica had left his life.

Left because he'd pushed her away, he thought. But he had done it, and now he had to live with it. There was no going back. He'd made sure of that. Burned his bridges behind him. Every damn last one.

And most likely burned his only real chance at happiness. Hindsight was a bear, mocking him even as it swiped a big, hairy paw at him, claws outstretched, saying "Too late."

"You finished tinkering yet?" he asked the mechanic who was making a timing adjustment on his sleek, gunmetal gray car. His latest toy.

"Almost."

Almost. Sounded like the adjective for his life, Logan thought. Almost happy, but not quite. Almost there, but not really.

Looking off into the cloudy horizon of Southern California, Logan shoved his hands into his pockets. It took him a second to realize they were clenched. He straightened his fingers out with a jerk. Usually he would have been the one doing the adjusting. Ever since he'd first hung around a racetrack, he'd had a natural feel for cars, a way with them that transformed them from complex machinery into extensions of himself. It was a knack he'd inherited from his late grandfather.

But lately, he was losing interest. Even his love for exhilarating speed wasn't enough to erase this inner turmoil he was constantly wrestling with. As the mechanic worked, Logan remembered another time, another place. It was evening, beneath a sky littered with stars, a night created just for him. And for Jessica.

Or perhaps created because of Jessica.

Her laughter had filled the air, making him feel a myriad of things all at once. So many emotions, so many feelings, all colliding into each other, taking possession of him. It had been frightening at the time, not to be able to control his own response to a woman who whispered along the perimeter of his mind like a light spring breeze filled with the heady perfume of first blossoms. Damn frightening, especially to a man who was so accustomed to controlling things.

Funny, nothing was ever the same again after she'd gone. Mornings and evenings were just that, mornings and evenings. Not beginnings or endings, not celebrations of life, just a continuation of what had gone before and would come after. Nothing special.

"She's ready, Mr. Buchanan."

Logan looked blankly at the mechanic. It took a moment before the words sank in.

"Right." He nodded at the man and slipped in behind the wheel. It was a perfect fit.

Just the way he and Jessica had been.

Logan swore under his breath. What the hell was the matter with him? *Was* it the letters that were doing this to him, causing him to reassess his life and come up short? They had nothing to do with Jessica, but somehow all the threats he read seemed to evoke thoughts of her. Reminding him that the greatest thing he could have had, he'd already lost. By his own design.

For a while, after the breakup, he'd seen one woman after another, trying to lock all thoughts of Jessica out. It had worked. For a while. But not now. Not anymore. He realized now that he couldn't fool himself indefinitely. She was still there, hiding in the shadows of his mind.

He had a feeling that she would always would be. Keeping him humble. Making him regret.

But that didn't change things. It was over and would have to stay over. Jessica's pride, he knew, would never allow anything else.

Turning the key, he couldn't blame her, much as he wanted to. He revved up the engine for his practice run.

Chapter 1

Who *was* he?

Jessica Deveaux had almost come out and asked point-blank when she first saw him, but the telephone repairman moving around in her third-floor office would have undoubtedly thought it was a come-on. So she kept the nagging question to herself.

Jessica sighed. She'd remember soon enough, probably when she least expected it. Everything was filed away in the recesses of her mind. As a private investigator, she never knew what tidbits or stray pieces of trivia could prove useful, and she was blessed with total recall.

It just didn't come every time she called, that's all, she mused, watching the man disappear into the outer office.

It was more his body than his voice or face, she

decided. There was something almost defiant about the set of his shoulders. Something that struck a distant chord. A chord that refused to yield an audible sound. But it would. In time. It would come to her.

"There," the repairman announced. "That should put you back in business."

Jessica blinked as she realized he'd come up beside her, holding out his work order for her to sign. Some detective she was, she thought, looking up. He gave her a quirky smile, waiting.

"I'll sign that," Albert announced, entering the room. The repairman frowned in annoyance as Albert pulled the clipboard away from Jessica.

Albert Tyler took his job as Jessica's secretary and office manager the way he took everything else in life: very seriously. With a flourish, he signed his name and handed the board, paper and pen back to the man, acting just like the queen's chief minister dismissing a servant, Jessica thought.

Just the vaguest hint of a scowl crossed the man's face before he nodded at Jessica and retreated, leaving the office.

Jessica stared after the repairman, then looked up at Albert. All six foot six of him. "Did he look familiar to you, Albert?"

"Page 1012 in the encyclopedia, under the telling heading of 'Neanderthal.'"

"Then he wasn't familiar to you." She sighed, wishing it wasn't eating at her this way. The repairman probably resembled someone she'd seen on television, or at a party. She had no idea why there was this feeling of uneasiness when she looked at the man. He seemed amiable enough, except when Albert got in his face.

"Never saw him before in my life," Albert replied crisply. His sharp gaze shifted to the pamphlets he'd brought in for her. The ones he'd insisted she look over. It was obvious she hadn't. "So, where are you going on your vacation?"

"Nowhere." She appreciated the fact that Albert took far more interest in her life than her own parents did, but fond of him though she was, she wasn't about to allow him to run her affairs for her. "I don't need a vacation, Albert."

She'd spent almost the first twenty years of her life on vacation, cocooned in her parents' jet-setting life. Now she was finally catching up, making up for lost time. Just because she was a little testy and worn around the edges the last few days didn't mean she needed to lie on some beach like an inert seashell.

Very carefully, Albert spread out the pamphlets she'd swept off to one side. "Well, you certainly need something. You're becoming impossible to live with these days."

Just as he'd opened each pamphlet, she closed them. "Don't bully me, Albert. I just need a stimulating case, that's all."

Albert halted his fruitless endeavor, temporarily giving up. He looked down a nose that would once have made a Roman patrician proud. "More like a stimulating man if you ask me."

Jessica raised her eyes to his. "I didn't ask."

Whether or not she asked made no difference to Albert, she knew. His theory was that some people needed to be helped despite themselves. He had thrown in his lot with her, and that meant looking out for Jessica even if she didn't want him to. "Cloistered nuns have a more active social life than you do."

The sad thing was that he was right, but she didn't want to hear about it. She would have killed to have the phone ring. Having wrapped up her last case Monday, except for a few loose ends here and there, she was painfully in between clients. And while money was never, and would never be, a problem for her, inactivity was. When she was inactive, she started thinking, and that wasn't good.

"Thank you for sharing," Jessica said with an edge. "Don't you have some file updating to do?"

Albert drew himself up and looked even taller than he was. And thinner. His burgundy sweater hung shapelessly around his frame. "Already done."

She felt the ends of her temper slipping away and did her best to hang on to them. "Then find something else to do, Albert. My social life is not your project of the month."

He began to ease out of the room, muttering, "More like of the year."

She looked at him sharply, struggling between anger and amusement. Albert *did* have her best interest at heart, she supposed. "I heard that."

He stopped, giving her a significant look. As if anything ever happened that he didn't intend to have happen. "You were supposed to."

The phone rang, answering her silent prayer. Finally, a moment of respite.

Albert went to answer the call.

Curious, Jessica waited, hoping that at the very least it wasn't a wrong number. Her office telephone number shared six digits with a local restaurant. On the average, she received five calls for reservations a week.

A moment later, her own phone buzzed. Instead of picking up, since the door leading out was opened, she called out to him. "Who's on the line, Albert?"

She heard the exaggerated sigh before he replied. "Someone you shouldn't talk to."

That was an odd answer, even for Albert. Jessica rose from her desk and crossed to the doorway. "Meaning?"

Albert looked at the telephone accusingly. "It's his brother."

"His?"

It was a completely impersonal pronoun that could be attached to the entire male population at large, Jessica thought. There was no reason in the world why adrenaline should suddenly be pumping itself through her veins in anticipation. Except that Albert, with his tendency to mother her, wouldn't be trying to shield her from the entire male population at large. Only from one male in particular.

Albert gave a little huff. "Dane Buchanan is on the line and says he needs to speak to you. Says it's—"

Jessica didn't wait for him to finish. Turning on her

heel, she was back in her office and leaning over her desk to pick up her receiver.

"Hello?"

"Jessica, it's Dane Buchanan."

Jessica sat down behind her desk again. She took a breath. She hadn't spoken to Dane since she and Logan had gone their separate ways. Why was he suddenly calling? "Dane, if this is a social call, I—"

"I'm afraid it's not a social call. It's business." Jessica heard tension enter the man's voice. "I know I don't have the right to ask, not after what happened between you and Logan, but I need to see you as soon as possible."

Her skin prickled, bringing her to attention. "Why, what's going on, Dane?"

"I guess there's no way to say this but to say it. Logan's been getting death threats."

She found that difficult to fathom. Logan had always led a charmed, golden life. "Disgruntled women?"

"I'm serious, Jessica."

Straightening, Jessica's hand tightened on the receiver. "Tell me."

"He's been getting these letters, incoherent things really, promising dire consequences unless—" Dane broke off the sentence, hesitating. "Listen, he'd kill me if he knew I was calling you, but he absolutely refuses to go to the police, won't take this seriously at all." Dane blew out a breath in exasperation. "Well, you know Logan."

No, not really. *I just thought I did.* Jessica swallowed the retort. "Yes, I know Logan. Nothing's serious as far as he's concerned."

"Jessica, I'd really appreciate being able to talk to you in person about this. It's pretty delicate. I'm not due in the office for another couple of hours. If you could just come by the house..." His voice trailed off, leaving a hopeful note in its wake.

She glanced at the calendar on her desk out of habit, knowing what she would see before she looked. The morning was completely free. She almost wished it wasn't, so she could offer an legitimate excuse. It wasn't in her to lie. One of her failings, she supposed, not being able to form gracious lies to ease herself out of difficult situations.

"All right." She checked her watch. At this hour there'd be no traffic. She gave herself a little extra time, anyway. "I can be there in about forty minutes."

"Perfect. And Jessica?"

There was something in his voice, she couldn't quite place it. She supposed, when it came to the Buchanans, she wasn't very good at second-guessing. "Yes?"

"Thanks."

"Don't thank me yet." She hung up and frowned at the receiver. It took her a moment to realize that Albert was in the doorway, disapproval etched into his angular features.

"You took the call."

"I took the call."

He huffed as he walked into the room. "It seems

that that repairman didn't get all the bugs out of the phone system.'' He pushed the telephone back on her desk with a disdainful hand. ''There should be a way to screen out the undesirables.''

Albert was getting a little too carried away, she thought. But then, he had a flair for the dramatic, and he did make her laugh. At times that was very, very important to her. And he had other valuable attributes. He could make a computer dance to his every whim.

Still, that didn't give him a right to be her censor. ''Dane Buchanan is not an undesirable.''

''No,'' he granted. ''But his brother is.''

She shook her head, a bittersweet smile playing along her lips. ''No,'' she said softly, ''that's just the trouble. He's not.''

Albert leaned forward, scrutinizing her face. ''You're not seriously thinking about taking this case, are you?'' He had his answer before the words were out of his mouth, but he was hoping he had misread her.

''And why wouldn't I seriously think about taking this case?''

''Because it's a sham, a ploy, a way to get you up there to see Logan.'' Surely she had to see that. She was as smart as they came, and a child could see this was a fabrication.

''A,'' she ticked off on her fingers, ''I'm seeing Dane, not Logan, and B, there is no ploy. I did not walk out on Logan Buchanan, he walked out on me. He doesn't want to 'get' me back.'' She pulled her purse out of the bottom drawer of her desk and kicked it closed again, punctuating her statement.

He knew all the details, had been there to hold her hand and call Logan vile names in her stead since she didn't vocalize her pain. He detested Logan for what he'd done to Jessica's heart.

"All the more reason for you to say no." He knew it was fruitless to tell her not to go. He tried, anyway. "You're too sharp a lady to walk into that lion's den and willingly let yourself be devoured."

Jessica laughed. "You are a very colorful man, Albert. No lion's den, no devouring, I promise." She crossed to the doorway. "I'm just going to listen for old times' sake, maybe give him the benefit of my advice. Chances are I won't have to see Logan at all. And I'll see you later."

He merely snorted his displeasure. "Be careful."

The warning rang in her ears. Jessica stopped, then turned around and took him by surprise by kissing his cheek. "Thanks for caring, Albert."

Albert touched his cheek, watching her go. "It's a dirty job, but someone has to do it."

"Yeah, yeah." She waved a hand at him as she went out the door.

No matter how much Jessica tried to deny it, to bury it, her stomach turned over with anticipation as she drove through the towering black gates after identifying herself to the man in the security booth.

Albert was right, she should have her head examined for even thinking about coming here, much less actually doing it. So why in heaven's name had she? Why wasn't she turning her car around instead of parking outside his house?

Because, she thought, shutting the car door behind her, heartless bastard that he was, if this was on the level, then Logan needed her. She knew damn well that he wouldn't go to the police. That wasn't his style.

Besides, if anyone was going to shoot Logan Buchanan, it was going to be her. She'd earned the right. In spades.

They'd met on a rainy day, much like this one. She'd looked like a drowned rat, dashing for the cover of the awning. Late for a fund-raiser she hadn't wanted to attend but had, at her mother's insistence. Jessica had collided with Logan and sent him sprawling. And he had laughed it off.

She'd always loved the sound of his laughter. Deep, rich, like a revitalizing cup of coffee.

And she'd loved him with all her heart. Her young, foolish, misguided heart. She hadn't given a single thought to self-preservation.

Being with Logan then had interrupted her life. She'd put everything on hold for him.

Jessica had been that sure he was the right one.

Well, he wasn't, and their relationship had taught her a valuable lesson. It had taught her not to trust her instincts. Sometimes the facts had to come into play. Facts such as the one that clearly showed Mr. Logan Buchanan was a man who dallied, then went on to the next amusement on his list. Usually a su-permodel with surgically enhanced lips and breasts.

Jessica shut her eyes, trying to squeeze away the memory. It was two years in the past. Better put, she was two years in the future.

Jessica turned toward the house. For one precarious moment her breath threatened to back up in her lungs as she saw him. Saw Logan rounding the side of the house she'd once told him could have easily doubled as the gracious Southern mansion in *Gone With The Wind,* even though it was in Southern California.

Rounding the side of the house and coming toward her.

He looked as surprised as she felt. He didn't know she was coming, did he? He hadn't secretly coached his brother to make the call.

Jessica realized that she was still holding on to that hope. Idiot.

Oh God, why had she come? And why wasn't she immune to the sight of him? Why, after all he'd put her through, after all the time that had gone by, did he look so damn good to her? Jessica decided then and there that there really was no justice in the world.

For a glimmer of a second, Logan thought he was hallucinating, that he'd crossed the line between re-ality and make believe. Was he now actually conjur-ing up images of Jessica instead of just imagining her in his mind's eye?

But she was real, and she was here.

She took his breath away. As always.

He'd come perilously close to totaling the car in

the practice run this morning. Something had gone
wrong with the steering column, and he'd narrowly
avoided flattening himself and his car against a wall.
The incident had managed to put the fear of mortality
in him like nothing else ever had.

Was it just a fluke, human error, or had whoever
was writing those letters to him just upped the ante
and taken those threats a step further?

The question had throbbed in his head until just
now, when he'd seen her.

Like a man in a dream, he continued walking toward her, expecting her to disappear at the last moment.

She didn't disappear.

This was no mirage, no hallucination. This was no
trick of light or mind. This was Jessica, looking even
more beautiful than he remembered. He hadn't
thought that was possible. Logan could feel an ache
starting in his gut.

Had she really thought she was going to come here
and not run the risk of seeing Logan? Jessica chided
herself. But wouldn't Dane have said something about
Logan being on the premises? Dane knew what had
happened between her and his brother, he would have
warned her.

Wouldn't he?

Mentally, she braced herself, knowing she'd been
through worse. But for the life of her, she couldn't
remember when.

Why hadn't she listened to Albert?

Logan stopped before her, still feeling like a man

trapped in a dream. Why was she here? He couldn't come up with a single plausible explanation, couldn't even think rationally. But then, she'd had that effect on him from the start.

He'd seen her once or twice since the breakup. In a crowd, at some social function or other. He'd kept his distance for both their sakes, mainly his. But now she was here on his home ground, and distance was the last thing that was crossing his mind.

"Jessica."

For the second time in Logan's life, he felt awkward. The first time had involved her, as well. It was when he'd watched her rush from his library, crying, after he'd told her it was time they went their separate ways. That they'd had a great run, but now the curtain was coming down and it was over.

He hadn't known what to do then, either.

She'd be damned if she'd stand here, frozen like some unschooled adolescent. Jessica raised her chin, her eyes narrowing slightly. Was it her imagination, or just wishful thinking on her part, that made him look just a little uneasy?

"You look like you've seen a ghost, Logan."

The smile was slow in coming. When it arrived, she knew that, a thousand oaths to the contrary, she wasn't any more immune to him now than she'd ever been. Just more intent on resisting.

Logan forgot all about the incident at the track. All about the death threats. He didn't know why she was here, and he didn't care. Those were all details that would somehow take care of themselves. He just wanted to look at her.

"The Ghost of Christmas Past," he answered, surprised that he could sound so calm when all he could think of was taking her into his arms and holding her to him. He knew he couldn't. He'd lost that right. And there wasn't a damn thing he could do about it. That would require begging forgiveness, and he didn't beg.

Even when he wanted to.

In spite of himself he ran his eyes over her, memorizing, remembering. "What are you doing here?"

Jessica reminded herself that this was the man who had ripped out her heart and then not even offered her a Band-Aid to stop the bleeding. It galvanized her resolve. She hardened her gaze.

"Funny, I was just asking myself the same thing."

There was fire in her eyes. He could remember when she felt like fire in his arms. An all-consuming fire. He missed that. Missed her.

"And what did you hear yourself answering?"

Her chin rose. "Save the charm, Logan. I'm not wet behind the ears anymore."

"As I recall, your ears were deliciously dry. And deliciously tempting."

Albert was right. It was a setup. She had no idea why, and for once, didn't want to solve the puzzle and find her answer. She just wanted to leave.

"And remarkably good at hearing things," she retorted crisply, promising herself she wouldn't lose her temper. "Like the word *goodbye.* If you'll excuse me," she said, turning to leave, "this was a mistake."

Mistake.

The word jumped up at him, hoary and full of nettles. He wanted to call to her, to tell her that *he'd* been the one to make the mistake, a horrible mistake that he was paying dearly for.

But the words wouldn't come out now any more than they had then.

The door behind him flew open, and he heard his brother call out, hurrying to stop her, ''Jessica, please, don't go. Come in.''

For once, Logan thought, his brother's timing and his words were perfect.

Chapter 2

Jessica paused on the bottom step, undecided. Though she tried to look only at Dane, she was acutely aware of Logan's presence. Blocking him out had never been an easy trick.

Go, get out now, while you still can, her mind begged her.

"I don't know, Dane. Maybe you'd better—"

Dane's eyes implored her to reconsider as he hurried down the three stone steps to her. Standing beside Logan, he seemed like a pale, unfinished version of his younger brother.

He spared one glance at Logan before taking Jessica's hand. "He was just leaving, weren't you, Logan?"

The smile that came to Logan's lips was slow, thoughtful. He didn't know what was going on, but he dealt himself in. "No, actually, I was just arriving."

Logan remained where he was, his eyes sweeping over Jessica. It was almost painful, he realized, being so close to her. The last thing he needed was pain.

"But I can be leaving again," he agreed amiably. "If that's what you want." The last sentence was addressed to Jessica.

Feeling a little as if he was hurling his body onto a field full of live ammunition, Dane placed himself strategically between Jessica and Logan.

"Maybe for now, you should." Dane smiled hopefully at Jessica. "If Jessica decides to help, she can always get to you."

"She already has," Logan murmured. Turning on his heel, he withdrew and disappeared behind the house.

But for Jessica, his words remained, hovering in the air, marking his place. Logan always knew how to make an exit. Knew just what to say to light a fire. She squared her shoulders. Or to dampen a flame. Jessica seriously doubted Logan had ever said an accidental word in his life.

Placing his hand on her elbow, Dane gently coaxed Jessica around and then up the steps leading into the house. For her part, she congratulated herself on not looking over her shoulder toward where Logan had disappeared, even though she was strongly tempted.

Dane closed the front door behind them. Jessica took a deep breath, bracing herself for the onslaught of memories. She'd spent too much time here not to encounter them.

"I really was going to leave, you know," she told Dane as he joined her, "just before you opened the door and came out."

Dane nodded. "I know." He indicated the library and began to lead the way. "Lucky for me I got there just in time."

He made her smile. She'd always liked Dane. But that didn't mean she was going to allow him to blindly lead her down the garden path.

"If you're trying to flatter me, Dane, don't. There's nothing I can do that a score of other detectives can't." She knew of several she could recommend, none of whom came with the history she did.

Once in the library, Dane began to close the door, then thought better of it. He remembered the night he'd seen her fleeing from this room, tears glistening on her cheeks. She hadn't seen him and he'd remained where he was until he'd heard the front door slam shut, unable to offer words of comfort. It was the only time he'd ever called his brother a damnable ass.

He left the door open, sensing she'd feel better that way. "I don't know about that," he contradicted politely. "You can stay close to Logan."

It was the last thing she wanted to do. And it was far from an exclusive trait. "Any hot little number wearing a size too small can do that."

The harsh note in her voice surprised her as much as it obviously did Dane.

"I never thought I'd see you bitter, Jessica. Did he hurt you that much?" he asked softly.

So much for keeping a poker face. Jessica raised her chin as she straightened her shoulders. She'd let her guard drop. That was inexcusable, even if Dane was an old acquaintance.

"Worse," she admitted. "I *let* him hurt me that much."

That was the worst part of it, that she had allowed Logan to break her heart when she'd known exactly what he, what men who dallied in this world she made her way through, were like. Her own father had had more mistresses, both during his marriage to her mother and after, than she could ever have hoped to keep track of.

Dane looked toward the door. "Maybe I had better—"

She shook her head, knowing what he was going to say. The last thing she wanted was to be the object of pity. It was coming back here that had made her momentarily lose control.

But she was all right now. Or would be once she reestablished a firmer grip on her emotions. If she couldn't separate her personal life from her professional one, she had no business doing what she did for a living.

"No, you were right to call me. And the best way to become immune to something is to take it in small doses until it has no effect on your system." She smiled. "Even works with some kinds of poisons."

If she was ever going to get over Logan, she had

to be able to face him and not feel anything. She couldn't do that by running away. And she couldn't live with herself if she ran. The "cure," the chance to finally be over Logan, had fallen straight into her lap, and she was going to make the most of it.

Dane studied her for a moment. "So you're interested?" he said, sounding hopeful.

The word was far too charged standing on its own, Jessica thought. "Let's just say I'm interested in listening."

Taking a key from his pocket, Dane unlocked the center drawer of the desk that had once belonged to his grandfather and opened it. "The letters are in here."

She watched him take out a manila file pocket. "How many and how often?"

"Four." He held the file pocket out to her. Jessica took out a pair of thin rubber gloves from her purse and pulled them on, before reaching for it.

"The first one arrived at work about two and a half weeks ago. I was in Logan's office and saw it on his desk," Dane recalled, then laughed shortly. "He was going to throw it out."

That sounded like Logan. Glancing at the postmarks, she sorted them by date. The envelopes had been handled too much to yield a clear set of prints, but there might be hope for the letters inside.

"But you wouldn't let him?"

Dane shrugged. "I take things more seriously than Logan does. You never know…" He let his voice trail off.

She knew what he meant. When you were wealthy and part of a prominent corporation that paid the salaries of thousands of people, a different set of ramifications came into play.

Opening the first envelope, Jessica quickly scanned the letter. "No, you never do."

She read all four letters out loud. Worded almost identically, they warned Logan of fatal consequences if he didn't throw his influence in on the "right side." They read like something out of a bad melodrama.

Folding the last letter, Jessica raised her eyes to Dane. "Right side?" she repeated. "And what side would that be?"

Dane looked almost uncomfortable at the question. "My side," he admitted. "There's going to be a stockholders' meeting at the end of the week to decide whether or not our company is going to merge with International Technologies."

Referred to as IT, International Technologies had its finger in too many fields for anyone but the government to keep track of. She knew her own father thought highly of the giant, as did his stockbroker. But this proposed merger was something new. "Oh?"

"There're a lot of advantages to the merger," he told her matter-of-factly. "A lot of people on both boards are eager to see it go through."

"You included." It wasn't a question.

He smiled. "Me included."

Dane was the businessman in the family, the brains. Up until now, she had thought that Logan's only involvement in the company business was to spend the dividends that were earned. "And Logan's against this?"

She couldn't think of a single reason why he'd oppose the merger. The Logan she knew never occupied himself with business, allowing Dane to handle it all. His position on the board was a sign of respect for his grandfather who had made the company what it was today—nothing more.

Dane shrugged. "He said something about keeping the company within the family. I think he was actually talking about the people who're working at Buchanan Tech right now. Some of them would naturally be let go with the redundancy of positions once the merger goes through." He saw the quizzical look enter her eyes. The same question had occurred to him. "I know it's a change. Logan was never that interested in the company to begin with. He was more into racing his cars and—"

"And finding how many women he could pack into a year, yes, I know." Fast cars and faster women, those were Logan's requirements. She had no idea how she had ever fit into his world. At the time, she'd thought she fit perfectly, but now she knew otherwise. Maybe he'd just been looking for a break. "What changed him?"

Dane weighed his words. "I'd say you leaving him was what started it."

Jessica looked at him sharply. "Then you'd be wrong." She struggled with the bitter taste in her mouth. "I had no effect on his life."

Dane shook his head. "I'm in a position to dispute that."

He was only trying to spare her feelings, Jessica thought. They didn't need sparing. They needed packing—in ice—until this was over. But she smiled at Dane for the sentiment he offered.

"You were always very sweet, Dane."

She looked back at the letters she'd spread out on the desk. There was no hope for a telltale broken key being struck over and over again. The day of the typewriter was gone. Technology made things a little tougher sometimes, she thought. Printed on a laser printer, the letters were all unremarkable and could have come from any one of a battalion of printers.

Jessica sighed and replaced each in its envelope, then tucked all the letters back into the folder.

She looked at Dane. "Is there anyone who would be particularly upset by Logan opposing the merger?"

"At least half the board members are counting on the merger going through."

She thought of her parents. The rich loved getting richer. "I'd like a list of their names."

Dane smiled and pulled out a folded piece of paper from his inside pocket. He held it out to her. "Way ahead of you, Jessica."

She took the list from him. Dane had always been the organized one. The thoughtful one. If she'd had any sense, it would have been Dane she'd fallen in love with, she admonished herself. Dane was sweet, patient, kind. All the right things.

But Logan had that extra something that could never be described, only felt, she thought ruefully. So Dane was the dependable one, and Logan was the one who set women's hearts on fire.

Didn't say much for the female population, herself included, Jessica mused, tucking the letters into her oversize purse.

She glanced over the list he had given her. There were over a dozen names. "Any thoughts on who might be resorting to scare tactics?"

"Do you think it's just that?" he asked hopefully. "Scare tactics?"

People did strange things where money was concerned, but in her estimation, it was always best not to let imagination get the best of you.

"This isn't the movies, Dane. I don't think anyone is going to rashly carry out any threats or take any wild potshots at Logan to sway his opinion." A pensive look came over his face. "What...?"

As if roused by her question, the look disappeared. Dane shook his head. "Nothing. I just hope you're right, that's all. But I still want you to look into this—" Dane's words were cut off by his pager. Apologizing to Jessica, he dialed the number shown on his beeper's screen.

Jessica distanced herself from him to give Dane some privacy. It was then that the room began to make an effect on her, moving from her unconscious awareness and taking center stage. The wave of emotion that suddenly reared up drenched her, threatening to steal her breath away.

This was where it had happened, she remembered. Where Logan had callously and cavalierly broken her heart without a single indication that he even knew or cared how devastated she was. He'd said goodbye to her in this room, saying something flippant about their having used up their allotted time together and that he felt it was time for him to move on.

Move on, as if she were some hotel room he was vacating for better, more interesting quarters.

As if she'd meant nothing to him when she'd been so sure that she had.

Jessica clenched her hands at her sides, shaking off the feeling.

When she heard him put down the phone, Jessica turned around to face Dane. The expression on his face was apologetic as he buttoned his jacket.

Dane nodded toward the telephone. "Duty calls. I'm afraid we're going to have to continue this discussion later today."

She didn't relish drawing this out any more than she had to. "I thought you said you didn't have to go in for a few hours."

His expression softened, making him more her friend than her client. He took her hand in his.

"Nothing is ever written in stone, Jessica." Dane looked at her for a long moment. "Nothing," he repeated. Releasing her hand, he picked up a briefcase that had been standing against the wall by the desk. "Listen, would you mind coming back tonight? Dinner, perhaps? As a favor to me? I'll send a car for you at eight." He saw the protest even as his words picked up speed. "I'll consider you on the case as of eight this morning."

That was even before she'd taken his call. She wanted no corners cut—and she really didn't want to be directly involved in this case. Jessica still thought that the best way to go would be for someone else to handle it for Dane. And for Logan.

"Dane, I—"

He'd obviously decided that he wasn't going to take no for an answer. Dane hurried out of the den. "Name your price, Jessica, I'll pay it."

"It's not a matter of money."

They both knew that. The spoon that had been in her mouth the day she was born was gold, not silver. Because of her grandparents on both sides and their trust funds, she didn't have to work a single day in her life if she didn't want to. It was only her stubbornness that had her "living in the trenches." Something her mother never tired of pointing out to her. It was right up there with her eternal lament that Jessica hadn't made "a suitable match" yet.

Heading toward the front door, Dane lengthened his stride as if to outrun her protest. "Good, then it's settled."

Jessica placed her hand on his arm. The touch was light but firm. He stopped reluctantly. "No, it is not. Don't railroad me, Dane."

"Sorry, it's just that I'm anxious for you to say yes." The look in his eyes implored her for the response. "Please, Jessica, I'm really worried about Logan. Granted, he's changed a lot, but my brother's still reckless when it comes to his own safety. He's not taking this matter seriously.''

She still couldn't imagine anyone carrying out the threat in letters. ''Maybe he shouldn't.''

Dane's expression was grave. ''And maybe he should.''

Jessica paused. Those would have been her words, if this wasn't Logan. *Should* have been her words, she reminded herself. Murphy's Law had a nasty habit of cropping up and biting you at the worst possible times. She was allowing her feelings to color her perception of the case.

Not very professional of you, Jess, she admonished silently.

Jessica slipped her hand from Dane's arm. ''You're right, maybe he should. Still, I don't think I'm the right person for the job—''

''On the contrary, you are the only person for the job,'' he insisted. ''You've got a good reputation and a good heart. That's enough for me.''

It hadn't been enough for Logan, she thought ruefully before she could shut the sentiment away.

As if he could read her mind, Dane looked into her eyes. ''Logan was a fool, but I figure you're woman enough not to hold it against him.''

She finally smiled as she relented. Maybe she'd intended to take this case all along. ''And I think Logan's not the only one who's good at sweet-talking in this family.''

Relief flushed out the concern on his face. ''Then you'll take it?''

She didn't believe in cutting off all avenues of escape. Just in case.

"For now," she allowed. "I'll start by checking out your security system."

"It's all state-of-the-art," he assured her. "See Neil at the gate." Neil, Jessica assumed, had been the man she'd met earlier at the security booth. "He'll walk you through it and answer any questions you have."

She smiled as Dane opened the front door. Everything still smelled wet from the early-morning rain, but the sun was finally trying to come out. "Can he answer why I've lost my mind and agreed to do this?"

"He might not, but I can." Stopping on the top step, he paused to take her hand in his. It was going to be all right, he thought. "Because you're the best, Jessica. I really appreciate this."

"Tell me that after you see my bill," she quipped. "All right, I'd better get to work."

Dane's smile widened.

"It's just a bunch of nonsense, you know."

Jessica didn't bother looking up from the security system schematic Neil had left her with, which was now spread out on the desk. She'd felt more than seen his shadow fall over her. Instantly she knew it had to be him.

Logan.

Even after all this time, she still had radar when it came to his presence.

Folding the paper carefully back up, she glanced in his direction. "Your brother doesn't seem to think so. He's really worried about you. Dane's willing to pay a lot of money to make sure this 'nonsense' doesn't have any repercussions."

"Dane always was a worrier." Like a man approaching the unknown, Logan carefully took a step closer to her.

Jessica held her ground, her chin lifting. If she didn't know better, she would have said there was an uncertainty about him. But that wasn't possible.

"Not like you, right?"

"No, not like me," he agreed softly, the words barely registering in his mind. He was too busy looking at her, exploring the feelings that were emerging.

Nothing had changed.

Everything had changed.

Logan took another step closer. Even as a child, he'd always liked challenging himself, always liked seeing how far he could push himself and still manage to come back from the edge.

He tapped the folded map in her hand. "The security system's state-of-the-art."

For a second she'd thought he was reaching out to touch her. She stilled the impulse to pull back. But she kept her voice cool.

"So Dane said. But there isn't a system around that can't be outmatched by someone."

"I guess nothing's perfect." He felt as if he were involved in some awkward dance, the steps to which he hadn't learned. Yet.

The look in her eyes was telling as she raised them to his. "No, nothing is."

Guilt skewered him with a long, sharp lance, running him through at the belly. Too bad he couldn't replay some scenes in his life. Redo them. Maybe things would be different now.

He longed to run his hand over her hair. Did it still feel like spun silk? "How have you been, Jessica?"

She was in no mood to pretend they were on good terms. And in no mood to pretend to believe he cared about the answer to his question. "I've been fine. Busy. Thank you for asking."

The short sentences were fired at him like pellets from a BB gun. He wasn't sure if he should be amused or brace himself for a larger assault. Probably the latter.

"Jessi," he began, having absolutely no clue what he was going to say.

She hated hearing him call her that, calling her a nickname no one else ever used but him. It dredged up too many memories. She wasn't here for memories, she was here to do a job.

Jessica cut in. "Has anyone been calling you, leaving threatening messages on your answering machine, following you? Anything like that, anything out of the ordinary?"

To the average man, Logan knew, his whole life was out of the ordinary.

"Just what you saw." He didn't want to waste either of their time with what would undoubtedly turn out to be just prank letters. "Listen, Jessi, I appreciate your coming here, but—"

"Whether you appreciate it or not doesn't concern me," she informed him coolly. "Your brother is paying me to ask these questions. Now, I'd like an answer."

He supposed he deserved the snub, but it stung anyway. And made him angry. Jessica was the only person who could ever make him experience a whole gamut of emotions.

"No, no phone calls, no one following me. Just what Dane probably showed you. Four rather uninteresting letters."

Uninteresting? Didn't he *feel* anything? Anything at all? "They threatened your life."

He laughed shortly. It was a dismissive sound. "It's a joke."

Her eyes darkened. "As I recall, everything was a joke to you, wasn't it?"

"Not everything." *You weren't,* he added silently. *I want another chance, Jessi. Another chance so I can try to make it right.*

Jessica stepped back when he reached for her. She knew that look and knew enough to be wary of it. She'd trod across the grounds and fallen into the pit once, but she knew where the holes were now, knew where all the land mines were located. She could make the trip from here to there and remain intact.

As long as he didn't touch her.

She thrust the security system schematic at him.

"Here, give this back to Neil." She picked up her purse. "I'll be in touch."

"Aren't you afraid someone'll shoot me while you're gone?" he called after her, only half teasing. He wanted to hear her answer.

"It's a joke, remember?" she reminded him.

It wasn't the answer he wanted. Without thinking, Logan hurried after her and caught her arm.

"Jessi, wait."

Jessica stood perfectly still, then turned her head slowly and looked down at his hand. When she raised her head, her eyes were cold and unfathomable.

"Let go of me." The words were emotionless and detached.

Logan dropped his hand and stepped back.

She didn't trust herself to say anything to him just now. Not until she managed to get her emotions under control. She'd underestimated her own feelings and come here seriously underarmed. That was hubris, but it wouldn't happen again.

Next time, she'd be prepared.

Jessica thought she heard Logan softly cursing to himself as she walked away.

It was a good sign, she told herself.

Chapter 3

Like the pillaging peasants running through the streets of Paris at the height of the Revolution, Jessica's emotions ran riot as she got behind the wheel of her car. She found herself jabbing her key into the ignition as she tried to ignore them. Seeing Logan again at such close quarters was a hell of a lot more difficult for her than she'd thought it would be. Seeing him and remembering the history that had gone down between them.

And the history that hadn't.

Her hands tightened on the wheel as it purred to life. Hopefully, she'd experienced the worst of it. Now she knew just how badly he could still unnerve her.

The trouble was, if she took this case, she knew she was going to have to listen to sporadic lectures about this, erupting from Albert's lips at the drop of a hat. It was a great deal to endure for someone she was trying to permanently work out of her system.

But beneath the wild fluttering at the pit of her stomach, she found something, deeper in her gut, that told her this was on the level. Logan was getting death threats, and he did need to be protected despite himself. He might think that he was above all this, but she knew better. People did ugly things when it came to money. And no matter what Logan thought, he wasn't invulnerable.

Jessica sighed as she guided her car through the gates and off the grounds.

He snapped to attention the instant he saw her car emerging between the two tall, imposing black gates across the street. It had taken her long enough.

He narrowed his dark eyes in concentration as she drove by, sliding down in the worn seat of his beige, nondescript car so that she wouldn't see him.

Not that she was looking for him.

Yet.

Smiling, he turned the key in the ignition, preparing to follow a discreet distance away. He was glad the rain had started again. It would help shield him.

A slow, mournful tune came from his tape deck as the current met it. A funeral dirge.

Fitting, he thought.

Excitement pumped through his veins. He turned the car around. It was beginning.

* * *

Albert jumped to his feet the minute Jessica walked into the outer office, his reflexes snapping to attention as if they were connected to the hinges of the door. One look at her flushed face had him scowling. He crossed to her quickly.

"My God, he's made you cry already."

She should have known Albert would think that. "No, he did *not* make me cry." Sniffing, Jessica tossed the crumpled tissue into Albert's wastebasket as she passed by it. "You know my sinuses always act up whenever the weather gets like this."

It annoyed her to feel anything but healthy. She didn't have the time or the patience to be sick. It only got in her way. She was never more content than when she was on the go, caught in perpetual motion. By design, she'd long since forgotten how to relax.

Exhaling, Jessica tried to compose herself. She dabbed at her eyes with another tissue, hoping the tearing would stop as suddenly as it started. She had to look like a sight to Albert. All in all, this wasn't shaping up to be one of her better days.

Jessica took the list of board members that Dane had given her out of her purse and handed it to Albert. "See if you and your magic computer can dig up the financial statements and any other useful information on these people."

Curious, Albert scanned the list quickly. The names meant nothing to him. He looked down at Jessica. "Who are they?"

"Members of the board of directors at Buchanan

Technology and IT—International Technologies,''
she elaborated when he stared at her blankly.

"Oh, *IT*."

Albert glanced at the list again. Anyone who read
the newspapers knew the front-runner in the aero-
space industry. International Technologies had been
in the news one way or another for the past five years.
Absorbing its competition like a giant, insatiable
amoeba.

He put the list on his desk next to his computer.
"Looking for anything in particular?"

Yes, a way to solve this quickly. She shrugged,
nonchalantly she hoped. "Maybe just a desperate person, maybe a possible murderer."

Reaching her doorway, she turned around to look
at him. For a second she debated telling Albert only
what was necessary and keeping the rest to herself.
But Albert was more than just a secretary. She relied
as heavily on him as she would have a partner. Maybe
more because she liked him.

"Someone is sending death threats to Logan."

Moving as bonelessly as he appeared to be at first
glance, Albert slid into his chair and turned the computer monitor toward him. His expression was completely innocent when he asked, "Would it be considered totally unethical to root for the other side for
a change?"

She didn't know whether to laugh or upbraid him.
She refrained from both. "Totally."

Albert pressed his lips together a second, as if

mourning the decision. They almost disappeared altogether. "Pity."

This time Jessica bit back a laugh. Good old Albert. At bottom, he was probably more loyal than most pets.

Though she knew there was probably a diatribe about this lurking somewhere and she was better off just retreating, vague curiosity had her pushing the envelope a little.

Leaning a shoulder against the doorjamb, she studied him. "Why do you dislike him so much, Albert? You never met the man."

Albert spared her a short glance before looking at the screen again. "I don't dislike him," he corrected crisply. "I loathe him."

How many people still used that word with a straight face? she wondered. "Why?"

With a click of a key, he loaded the program he wanted. "Because you never got over him."

She knew Albert was just being protective, but there were times when he got a little too carried away. Like now. She didn't like the assumption he made. It was too close to the one haunting the perimeters of her mind.

"I get over everything, Albert. Colds, flu and Logan Buchanan."

Albert didn't bother looking up from his computer screen. His fingers flew across the keyboard as if they had a life of their own. Quite possibly, she mused, they did.

"Then why," he asked, his voice accusingly low,

"aren't you on a cruise ship right now? Why do you insist on getting yourself involved in this instead? God knows you don't need the money."

"Because working is far more interesting than lying around." She loved pitting herself against puzzles and mysteries, loved putting the tiny, broken pieces together to form a clear whole. She'd had a natural aptitude for it and gravitated to criminology in college. Becoming a private investigator seemed inevitable to her.

"A lot of people would argue with you about that."

Though Albert rarely mentioned anything about his past, she sensed that initially they came from two very different worlds. In some ways, hers had been just as trying as his. "A lot of people weren't made to feel like nonfunctioning ornaments for the first two decades of their lives."

She might not know much about Albert's world, but he knew a great deal about hers. She'd shared most of it with him willingly, albeit piecemeal. She knew he couldn't argue with her about this.

Jessica withdrew to her office. "I'll leave you to do what you do best."

She heard him mutter something under his breath, but thought it best to let it go. Probably just another disparaging remark about Logan.

In the three years since Albert had come to work for her, they had struck up a strong if somewhat strange relationship. Albert was part secretary, part den mother, part older brother, and invaluable in all three capacities. In general, he behaved more like a member of the family than an employee.

She opened the bottom drawer and deposited her purse. More honestly, Albert behaved the way she imagined family members who cared about one another behaved. She'd never experienced having a warm, caring family firsthand, so she could only speculate when it came to Albert's behavior toward her. Her mother had always been dedicated to the institution of marriage, so much so that she ventured into it every chance she got, each time with a progressively younger man than the last. Her father, on the other hand, shunned marriage altogether. He was dedicated to securing and enjoying the charms of as many mistresses as physically possible.

That had left very little time for her in either of their lives. Filial concern, except for a doting paternal grandmother who had died when she was eight, was something Jessica had very little knowledge of.

That was probably what had made her so vulnerable to Logan when she had fallen in love with him. Faced with what she thought was love for the very first time in her life, she'd had no natural immunities to fall back on. No defenses to draw on. There'd been no one to educate her that at times love came with thorns the size of roadside construction cones.

She knew now.

Opening up the large notebook that contained the very essence of her life within its overflowing pages, she began making notes to herself regarding Logan's case. She'd barely gotten to the third page when voices coming from the outer office caught her attention. Curious, Jessica laid down her pen and scooted her chair back to get a clear view of the doorway.

A delivery boy, hardly out of his teens by the looks of him, was just leaving. She didn't remember telling Albert to order anything.

"Who was that, Albert?"

Rather than answer, Albert walked into her office. He was carrying a long, white florist box in his arms.

"These are for you," he said, setting the box down on her desk, he opened his hand. "And so are these. Sinus medicine," he elaborated when she stared at the two white gel capsules nestled in his palm.

Jessica raised her eyes skeptically to his. "You just happened to be carrying around sinus medicine?"

He lifted a single thin shoulder and let it fall. It seemed to rustle, lost beneath his loose fitting sweater. "I believe in being prepared." He took a step toward the doorway, saying, "I'll get you a glass of water for the pills."

Jessica sneezed before she could say thank you.

"While I'm at it, I'll make you some tea." About to leave, he eyed the box he'd just brought in. "Do you want a vase for those, or will you just be throwing them in the trash, where they belong?"

She slid the bright red ribbon from the box, noting the name on the lid. Giovanni Gardens. Expensive. She dropped the ribbon on the side. "Why would I throw them out?"

The frown made his thin face appear austere. "Because they're undoubtedly from him." There was no mistaking who Albert was referring to. "Obviously he's started his campaign to weasel his way back into your affections."

Albert succeeded in making her laugh again. "Weasel is the last furry creature one thinks of when thinking of Logan Buchanan. Just get me a vase, thanks," she said as she lifted the lid from the box.

Sliding back the green tissue paper, she stopped to admire the lush pink roses lying beneath. She touched one, sliding her fingertip down the soft petal. Pink roses had always been her favorite. She wondered if he'd remembered, or if it was just luck.

Probably the latter. She sincerely doubted she'd left enough of an impression in his life for him to recall her favorite flower.

Were they the fragrant kind? she wondered. There was nothing she loved better than the scent of roses.

Jessica reached in to scoop the flowers out and felt something sharp rip into her fingers. The sudden gasp of pain was involuntary as she pulled her hands out quickly. Something sharp ripped at her fingers again as she did so.

Blood was dripping from three of them.

Albert came hurrying into the room, carrying a vase. Water sloshed from it. Like two brown shiny marbles, his eyes darted from her to the roses then to her fingers.

"What happened?"

A drop of blood fell on the white box. She pressed her thumbs to her fingers to keep from dripping on the desk. "I thought they took the thorns off roses when they sent them."

Albert snorted as he set the vase down. "Obviously the man wanted roses sent that fit his personality. I've got peroxide in the bathroom."

Leave it to Albert. "Of course you do."

He pointed toward the ceiling as he hurried out of the room for the peroxide. "Hold your hands up over your head." It was a direct order.

"This isn't a stab wound, Albert. I just have a few scratches." Scratches that stung like the devil, she thought.

Annoyed, she turned the box upside down, smearing blood on the sides as she dumped the flowers out on her desk. She wasn't about to risk getting impaled again.

Tumbling out along with the roses were what looked like three thick bougainvillea stems. Each stem had thorns along it that were thick enough to be used as medieval weapons of torture.

There was a small envelope stuck on one of the thorns. Carefully, Jessica pried it loose, then slit the envelope open, leaving a splotch of blood imprinted on it.

The single line on the white card inside could have come from the same printer that had spewed out Logan's death threats. It probably did.

"I can get to you at any time."

A cold shiver shimmied down her spine.

Jessica slipped the card back into the envelope just as Albert returned.

Noticing the envelope, he deposited peroxide, cotton balls and Band-Aids on her desk. His eyes widened when he saw the bougainvillea stems. "He send his calling card along?"

She supposed there was probably no point in having the envelope and card examined for prints, but maybe the sender had gotten careless and licked the envelope. DNA was almost as good as prints once they narrowed the list of suspects down.

Jessica let the envelope drop on her desk. "Logan didn't send these, Albert."

Albert dabbed peroxide on a cotton ball then swabbed it across her fingers. "You're probably right.... Then who did?"

"My guess is that it's the same person who's been sending death threats to Logan." At least, that seemed like the logical assumption. "Whoever it is probably wants to scare me off the case." She frowned. "How did he or she find out so fast?" It didn't make any sense. She'd only talked to Dane and Logan.

"Maybe 'he or she' didn't," he said, mimicking her tone. "Maybe it's just a hoax, and Buchanan's doing this to throw you off."

Logan might have broken her heart, but she didn't believe he was capable of inflicting physical pain. Jessica pulled back her finger, taking a Band-Aid from Albert and finishing the job herself.

"Look at those stems." She nodded at them, taping up the second finger. "They're practically lethal." Gingerly, she picked up the roses and began placing them in the vase one by one. "If I wasn't convinced that this was on the level before, I am now."

Albert sighed with resignation. "You're keeping them?"

She smiled, arranging the last rose. "Why not? They're pretty. Maybe looking at them will give me an idea." Pushing the vase to one side, she gingerly deposited the offensive stems back into the box, then slid the lid over it before handing it to Albert. "Put that somewhere for the time being. We might want it later. Then get back to the list, Albert. I want every scrap of information you can find on those people. There's got to be a clue somewhere."

As for her, Jessica thought, she was going to call the florist on the off chance that whoever sent these to her got careless and left something for her to go on.

Albert sighed and retreated from the room.

Sitting down at her desk again, she looked thoughtfully at the roses. Something didn't feel right, but she couldn't put her finger on it...stabbed or otherwise, she mused wryly, looking at the Band-Aids on her fingers. She pulled the telephone to her and dialed 411 to get the number of Giovanni Gardens.

"What happened to you?" Logan asked, letting her in after she rang the doorbell.

He'd waited for her to arrive, cursing himself for feeling like a damnable schoolboy with perspiring palms, anticipating his first tryst. But upbraiding himself didn't change the way he felt. Anxious. When the

limo he'd sent had returned without her, Logan was
sure she wasn't coming, despite the driver's assurance
that Jessica had told him she was driving herself over.

Once she'd arrived on his doorstep, he had to struggle not to look as pleased as he felt. He'd rushed her
last time. Rushed both of them. And then it had all
blown up on him. This time the steps he'd take would
be slow, sure. For both their sakes.

But seeing she'd been hurt, he took one of her
hands gently in his, studying her fingers, ignoring the
new accessories she was sporting.

He *would* immediately hone in on the negative, Jessica thought with resigned exasperation. She pulled
her hand away.

Though she'd told herself not to, she'd spent more
than a few minutes getting ready for this meeting over
dinner. She was going for the careless, knock-'em-
dead look. Obviously she could have saved herself
the time if all he was going to do was look at the
Band-Aids on her fingers.

She turned to look at him in the foyer, wondering
why Dane or even the housekeeper, Julia, weren't
there. She felt like a tightrope walker, just beginning
her journey along the long, thin wire with a forty foot
drop beneath her. "Someone sent me a box of roses
today."

Moving behind her, Logan coaxed the raincoat
from her shoulders. It was slightly damp. "Didn't the
florist take off the thorns?"

She didn't like him doing that, taking her coat. It

felt too much as if he were undressing her. Memories whispered along her mind. She shut them away.

With a jerk, Jessica freed herself of her coat and turned to face him. "Yes, but someone added bougainvillea stems."

Confusion melted into anger as he reached for her hand again. "Who the hell—?"

Jessica stepped back, pulling her hand back to her side. "My guess is, the same person who's been sending you your little missives."

Her call to the florist had yielded nothing, just as she'd thought. According to the clerk, the flowers had been purchased by an "average-looking man" who wasn't too tall, wasn't too short and had paid cash, hence destroying any hope for a paper trail.

Jessica looked around, trying not to be obvious. Where *was* Dane? "Obviously they don't want anyone poking around, trying to uncover their identity."

With a decisive movement, Logan hung her coat on the ornamental coatrack his father had brought back from Japan the year before Logan was born. "You're off the case, Jessica."

Her chin went up. There was a time she would have hung on every one of his words, listening without question. But she wasn't in a love-induced coma anymore. That woman no longer existed.

"You have no right to tell me what to do," she reminded him coolly.

He'd always admired her determination, but it had never been turned against him before. Anger flared, swiping the tip of its red-hot flames over him.

"You want to play games? Okay, we'll play games. I'm your client—"

She raised herself up on the balls of her feet, a fighter ready to go all the rounds necessary to win the championship match.

The word rankled her, rubbing her raw. "No, I do *not* want to play games. Logan. You might, but I don't. I never had time for games. And even if I did you wouldn't be the one I'd play with. You can't get the rules straight."

"What are you talking about?" he shouted back. Conscience pricked at him. Logan knew she wasn't talking about the case. She was talking about them. He didn't want to go there.

"Your brother is my client." She pointed the fact out tersely. "You're just the object of his concern."

Looking around again, Jessica caught her reflection in the hall mirror. She didn't look like a woman on pins and needles. But she was. Jessica silently congratulated herself on being able to keep her feelings from registering in her eyes.

"Speaking of Dane, where is he?" she wanted to know. He was supposed to be here. She never would have agreed to come otherwise.

"He's not here." Getting his temper under control, Logan indicated the way to the dining room. As if she hadn't gone there at least several dozen times before. "That emergency call that dragged him away from you earlier today—"

"Yes?" Jessica had a sinking feeling she knew what was coming.

"It turned out to be a more complicated situation than he initially thought."

She turned to look at Logan. The smile on his face answered her before she even asked the question. "Then it's just you and me for dinner?"

"Apparently."

That wasn't what she wanted to hear.

Chapter 4

The line about discretion being the better part of valor played in her mind.

It might be good advice, at that, Jessica decided. She glanced over her shoulder toward the door. Outside, thunder was rumbling, but nothing was happening yet.

The same couldn't be said for inside. The foyer, spacious and grand, seemed to be shrinking around her, and the light that cascaded from the chandelier appeared to be growing dimmer.

It wasn't panic she felt, it was her sense of self-preservation warning her that remaining here with Logan might be far from the best move on her part.

As a matter of fact, it might just be the worst.

She wondered how she could leave without making it seem like an out-and-out retreat.

"Maybe I'd better come back another time, when Dane's here."

There was a time when Logan could read everything she was thinking in her eyes. Now that way was closed off to him. He took a chance, remembering that she always rose to a challenge.

"Afraid?"

Jessica's eyebrow arched as her eyes narrowed. "Of what?"

"Of the ghosts between us." Because he felt them. Shimmering there beside them. The ghosts of what they'd once meant to each other were as real to him as if they had breadth and substance.

Was he actually mocking her? After all this time? She couldn't tell, but she felt her temper rising, anyway. Jessica clung to it as if it were a magic carpet that would fly her out of this dangerous place she found herself emotionally inhabiting.

"There aren't any ghosts, Logan. For there to have been ghosts means that something had to have been alive and thriving and then died. There was nothing alive between us." She'd believed that there had been, but he'd shown her she was wrong. Her eyes pinned him as she added, "It was all a misunderstanding."

The words hurt, though he told himself they didn't. She'd developed spunk, Logan thought. He liked it even if it was at his expense.

He half laughed to himself. "Well, I guess that's putting me in my place."

"I doubt if anyone could do that." He was in her

way. When she took a step, he matched it, blocking her way with his body. Jessica frowned. "Now, if you let me pass, I'll just get my coat and—"

But he wasn't about to let her leave so easily. He wanted her to stay. More than he'd believed possible. The same nerves that had danced their way into existence when he'd been waiting for her now reappeared for another performance.

Maybe it was borrowing trouble, but he found himself a petitioner.

Resting his hand lightly on her shoulder, he restrained her efforts. "Just because Dane isn't here doesn't mean that the death threats aren't."

So now he was playing the other side of the street? "I thought you didn't believe in the threats."

He shrugged. Ever so subtly, exerting a little pressure with his hand on her shoulder, he changed her direction. "Maybe I do and maybe I don't."

Something in his voice caught her attention. Her annoyance slipped away. Logan wasn't trying to be cagey. She knew him too well to be fooled. Something had gone down to change his mind.

"What happened?"

For a split second he thought of laughing the whole thing off. But that wouldn't keep her here. And maybe saying it out loud would remove the specter of what was bothering him about the incident.

"I'm not sure, really, but I think someone tampered with my car." She looked at him sharply. "The one I race," he clarified.

Jessica felt her heart constrict. Damn it, he'd been too cavalier about this. "When?" she demanded.

He scarcely recognized her. She'd snapped the question out at him. The Jessica he remembered had been quieter.

"This morning." He gave a boyish grin, trying to banish the serious topic to a nether region. "I barely avoided becoming intimately acquainted with a tree."

He could grin at her all he wanted. Jessica wasn't about to allow herself to get sidetracked. This was his life they were talking about.

"After I left?"

He shook his head. "Before you got here."

His answer almost left her speechless. "Then why didn't you tell me?" And then, when Logan didn't say anything, she filled in her own answer. "Because you thought you could handle it on your own?"

It wasn't really a guess. She knew him well enough to know the way he thought. The man never thought of fatal consequences. He thought himself invincible.

Logan resented her tone of voice. "I always have."

"Why is it that you could never admit that you needed help? That you needed someone?" Without realizing it, she clenched her hands at her sides. She regretted it instantly. Her cut fingers ached.

This wasn't the conversation he'd meant to have with her. The steps he wanted to retrace with Jessica involved candlelight and soft music, not the baring of souls and motives.

But she was waiting for the truth, and he knew

she'd leave if he didn't give it to her—at least in some measure.

"Because the minute you need someone, you're opening yourself up to disappointment. The only person you can always count on is yourself."

She hadn't thought, after all this time, that his words could hurt her. But they did. Damn it, he could have counted on her for anything, if he'd only been receptive enough to realize that.

Which one of them was the bigger fool, she wondered. Him for not knowing, or her for hanging on?

But this wasn't about her, or them, any longer. "Seems to me you can count on Dane."

"I can," Logan agreed. "But I don't." And therein lay the difference. They were closer than most brothers in some ways. Logan knew Dane was as loyal as a brother could be. And Dane did worry about him, about his safety, even if they were on opposite sides of the table on this one.

Jessica shook her head. How lonely and isolated that made him sound. "Were you always this cold and I just didn't notice?"

When they'd been together, he remembered, cold was the last word that came to mind.

"It's not cold, it's called a principle of survival." He paused, then because it was Jessica and he'd been as open with her as he could be with anyone, he allowed himself to say a little more. "My father trusted everyone and wound up getting burned all the time." He laughed shortly, thinking of the alimony lawyers that came to their door with regular frequency. His father never made a match that could stick. "Not to mention almost going bankrupt before my grandfather stepped in."

A gruff tyrant, his grandfather had never let his father forget that he bailed him out of his difficulties. Logan supposed that was one of the reasons his father drank. To blot out a world that hurt, as well as to obliterate the memories of his own shortcomings.

Jessica was well acquainted with Arthur Buchanan's history. There'd been as many women in the man's life as in her father's. The difference being that her father never released his hold on his heart while Logan's father gave it away for a song each time.

Of the two men, Jessica had always liked Logan's father better than her own. At least Arthur Buchanan was a warm, feeling individual.

"There's a difference between putting your trust in someone and trusting everyone who crosses your path," she said softly.

Logan's eyes held hers. She'd become more beautiful in her self-assurance, he realized. A longing twisted within him that he strove to ignore. "Are you telling me to put my trust in you?"

Once, I would have begged you to do that. "To do my job, yes."

That sounded so cold, but Logan couldn't fault her for it. It was exactly what he deserved. Still, he wanted her to remain. At least for the evening, if not more.

"Do you have to do your job on an empty stomach?"

"What?"

He placed his hands on either side of her shoulders, and she had to struggle not to let the heat of his hands seep into her being. She wished he hadn't taken her raincoat, although that was only cloth. Armor plating would have worked better.

"Stay for dinner, Jessi. Maxine worked hard to prepare everything you liked." When he'd gone to the cook with a list of what he wanted, the woman had taken one look at it before asking him if Jessica was coming. "She was very happy when I told her that you were coming for dinner."

A little bit more of the past nudged itself forward. Jessica remembered the woman well. Built like a line backer in drag, the woman had one of the most acidic tongues she'd ever encountered. But for some unknown reason, they had hit it off almost instantly. Supremely gifted in the kitchen, the grandmother of three could make a rock taste like a piece of culinary heaven.

Somehow Jessica thought that the woman would have moved on. "Maxine's still here?"

He laughed. "Where would she go? Who would she ever find to put up with all her eccentricities?"

He was right. There wasn't much of a market for a cook who towered over most men, sported several tattoos along the visible length of her body and spoke her mind. Most people went with first impressions. Luckily his father had been convinced to give her a try. Luckily, because Maxine and Julia, their housekeeper, were the only two women who remained con-

stant in Arthur Buchanan's life, tending to him until
his death.

"Besides—" Logan grinned, lightly placing his
hand to the small of her back and guiding Jessica to
the dining room "—she knows how I like my eggs."

Jessica remembered the large breakfasts Logan was
partial to. He'd always woken up ravenous and
couldn't understand how she could just get by on a
cup of coffee until she'd been up for several hours.
"You never did eat healthy."

Logan held out the chair for her. "Haven't you
heard?" As she sat down, he pushed in her chair.
"Eggs are no longer banished from our table. They're
back in favor." He leaned over her chair, his face
close to hers. "What are my chances of following in
their footsteps?"

His breath slid along her skin, a whispered re-
minder of the lover he'd once been. It wasn't easy
sounding unaffected, but somehow she managed.

"A, eggs have no feet, hence no footsteps. B, you
were never banished, you went into exile of your own
accord. And C, you were never considered high in
cholesterol." She looked at him pointedly as he took
his seat. "Just a high risk all around, and you did turn
out to be that."

"Ouch."

As if her words could have the slightest effect on
him. "Don't pretend, Logan. Nothing I could ever say
would leave a single mark on you."

His eyes held hers for a long moment. When he

finally spoke, his voice was unusually soft. "Don't be so sure, Jessi."

The look went straight to her heart, threatening to melt it.

Been there, done that, Jessica told herself sternly, shoring up the breach.

"I'm not here to relive old times, Logan." Picking up her fork, she jabbed at the salmon almondine in front of her as if it had somehow offended her. "I agreed to come to dinner because Dane said he'd fill me in some more on the situation. Since he's not here, the ball's in your court."

Logan frowned. "There *is* no 'situation,' Jessica," he insisted.

He only called her Jessica when he was annoyed, or being formal. She didn't care for either. "I saw the letters, Logan."

"I'm not talking about the letters. I was referring to your wording." Logan shrugged carelessly. "Or maybe it's Dane's wording." Until the last year, he'd always left the business end up to Dane, and he knew Dane had grown accustomed to speaking for both of them. Opposing him on the merger had really rattled his brother. Logan sighed. "Dane thinks I should back him in his position, and I think he's wrong."

Jessica picked up her wineglass. The contents gleamed in the candlelight. She watched the light skim off the top. "To think you should back him, or in his stand?"

"Both." Lifting his own glass, he silently toasted her before taking a large swallow. On rare occasions, like tonight, he longed for something with a kick to it. But maybe sitting opposite her here like this was kick enough. "Brothers can take opposing views. It doesn't mean they're any less of a family." That was his take on the matter, but Dane didn't quite see it that way. "He can't understand why I don't just throw my lot in with his, make him happy and put a stop the death threats, to boot." He drained his glass. "Make it simple all around."

Jessica had never known him to take up a cause before. It was a side of him she'd never known existed. He'd always been the playboy before, unwilling to be encumbered by mundane details.

"Why don't you?"

Why didn't he? A year ago he might have asked himself the same question. But that was before his father had died, and he'd seen how empty a life could be and how little significance the passing of that life could mean. It made him realize that he'd been wasting time. He had to make his life count for something.

The death threats he'd been receiving just intensified that feeling.

Logan reached for the bottle and topped off her glass before partially refilling his own. But rather than drink, he toyed with the stem. "Because I don't think that it's in everybody's best interest to let the merger go through."

"Dane seems to think it is."

His mouth curved. This time he sipped thoughtfully, watching her as he spoke. "Dane is the businessman in the family. He sees everything in terms of the bottom line. And the bottom line is money. For him.''

''But not for you?'' It had been while they were together. He'd never seemed to give a care as to how lavishly he spent it as long as it was there.

She was probing. Turning questions around on him. He didn't like being held under a microscope. ''Did you get your basic training from a psychiatrist?''

Oh no, she wasn't going to have him clam up. He didn't have that luxury, not if he wanted her to remain. ''Don't shift gears on me now by changing the subject. Why isn't money the bottom line for you?''

''Maybe because I don't need it,'' he guessed. If he had to earn it by the sweat of his brow, maybe it would be. Which was why he was taking the position he was. ''But other people do. Like the people this merger will be putting out of work.''

He could tell by the look in her eyes that Dane hadn't really gone into this at length with her. That was because his brother chose only to see the positive side to any given problem, not the negative.

''There's going to be a large redundancy of jobs if Buchanan Tech allows itself to be absorbed by IT. About a thousand people'll be out of a job so that stock values can rise.'' Sarcasm echoed in his voice. ''I don't know, doesn't seem very fair to me.'' He noticed her reaction. ''You're smiling.''

She hadn't realized that she was. ''That's not a smile, that's a stunned expression.'' Setting the glass down, she looked back down at her meal. She was beginning to find her appetite. ''Since when have you

taken to championing the little man?'' There was a
hint of humor in her eyes when she glanced up at
him. ''Don't tell me you've finally had exploratory
surgery, and they managed to locate your heart for
you.''

A tinge of conscience nettled him. He supposed
that in her point of view, he had seemed pretty heartless. Maybe he had been.

''I've done some growing since my father died.''

''I'm sorry about his death.'' She'd sent her con-
dolences when she read the obituary in the newspaper, but refrained from attending the funeral. She
hadn't wanted to be put in a position to feel Logan's
pain, no matter what she thought about him. ''Your
father was a good man.''

''He was a disappointed man,'' Logan corrected.
''That bit about putting his trust in the wrong people
went in spades when it came to the wrong women.
He had his heart dragged around a lot.''

''Maybe he just never found the right woman,''
Jessica suggested.

No, Logan thought, his father never did. ''He was
too eager to have someone to really make an effort
to be discerning. He settled on the first woman who
crossed his path and smiled at him, each and every
time.'' In a way, Logan supposed, he could relate to
the difficulty his father had encountered. Maybe it
wouldn't have made any difference if he had been
discerning. ''When you're rich the way my father
was, you find that a great many women smile at you.''

They shared that insecurity, Jessica thought. Never

knowing whether they were being approached for themselves or because of who and what they were. Only with their own kind, their own circle, was there a degree of ease. And even then, it wasn't always safe. For the rich, the desire to become even richer was not unknown.

Jessica thought of all the times she'd seen Logan's photograph in the society pages, always with someone new, someone different. "You'd know more about that than I would."

He was quick to be defensive. "You've had your share since…" Realizing what he almost said, he trailed off.

"I've been too busy working to have my 'share.' But if the newspapers are any indication, you've more than made up for my lack of playing the field."

He knew what she thought of him and was tempted to just let it go at that. But something within him wouldn't allow it.

"You know what those photographers are like. They're there to snap your picture from the minute you get up until you finally call it a night."

He could thrive on next to no sleep for days. She'd often wondered where he got his energy. "They must put in a long day with you."

He reached for his glass again, then decided not to. That had been his father's choice of an anesthetic, not his. Besides, he'd gone so long without her, he even savored the barbs.

"Your tongue's gotten sharper since we were together."

She raised her chin without knowing how much she aroused him when she did that. ''A lot of things have gotten sharper about me since we were together.''

Jessica was bluffing and hoped he was buying. However much she'd deluded herself into thinking she was over Logan, it was just that. A delusion. He seemed the same as he ever was, except more so. More charming, more sexy, more irresistible. More.

And yet, there was a sadness to him that she'd never seen before, which, she supposed, undoubtedly had its roots in his father dying so unexpectedly. Death left an indelible mark. Jessica thought of the death threats. She didn't want anything happening to him.

Leaning over her plate, she looked at him, forcing herself to think of Logan only as a case, a person she was being paid to help and nothing more. He deserved her undivided attention, her undivided professionalism. That didn't mean having her mind wander like this.

It was hard, though, keeping it bridled. She should have insisted on seeing Logan on neutral territory. Somewhere where they'd never been.

A smile crept to her lips. That probably meant the public library. In the nine months they'd spent together, they had gone almost everywhere. Made love almost everywhere. From the floor of his private jet to the last row of an empty Dorothy Chandler Pavilion after the L.A. Philharmonic Orchestra had given an exclusive performance. It'd been a fund-raiser, and they had secretly stayed behind after everyone else had left.

It had been one of the most exhilarating and memorable nights of her life.

Making love with Logan had always been an adventure. Each and every time. It would have been the same, she realized, looking into his eyes, had it happened in a six-by-nine room. Or a broom closet. Being with Logan was all that she'd needed.

She shook her head, freeing her mind of the web that was swiftly tightening around it. "So, does that mean that changing your mind about this merger is strictly out of the question for you?"

It wasn't so much about changing his mind; he'd done that often enough.

"Being a coward is out of the question," he informed her. "Even if I didn't believe as strongly as I do about what the merger would do to a lot of people working for Buchanan Tech, I wouldn't back down now. I'm not going to have someone think they can just threaten me and I'll fold."

Anyone who knew Logan knew he wasn't capable of that. The sender had to be desperate. Or almost a complete stranger.

But it was his attitude that intrigued her now and raised questions in her mind. "What happened? You never used to care about the company that made it possible for you to live the high life on any continent that suited you."

He shrugged. "People change."

That didn't cut it. "Not you."

He smiled. "Even me. Everybody's always rushing to make something newer, better, bigger. Maybe it's time we stopped once in a while to enjoy what we have instead of getting caught up in what we could get, and exclude everything else around us."

She was almost able to believe him. But believing him had been her fatal error. "My God, I'm impressed. You do have a heart. Or a glimmer of one." He reached across the table and put his hand over hers. Her smile faded as she withdrew her hand. "And I have a memory. A very clear one."

"So, where do we go from here?"

She picked up her fork again. "After dinner you get to tell me about anyone you think might have sent those letters to you."

Logan shook his head. "I'm not talking about the case."

"But I am. The only way this is going to work is if we leave the past where it is, Logan. In the past." Her eyes pinned his. "Understood?"

"Understood."

But something in his voice told her it wasn't.

Chapter 5

If she wanted proof that they hadn't reached an understanding, it wasn't long in coming.

It came almost immediately, following Logan's comment that Dane had become obsessed with his work, especially since their father's death.

To some extent, she knew that Dane had always been dedicated to work. The brothers were poles apart that way. "Nobody could ever accuse you of being a workaholic."

Logan took no offense. He couldn't. It was true. "Good old Jessica, always cutting to the heart of the matter."

He looked at her for a long moment, old feelings sending out long, wispy trailers to ensnare him. He'd fought them off once, and his immediate instincts were to retreat again. Instead, he let them come. And savored the sight of her.

It had been a long time. There were times when he'd actually thought he was over her. And then something would come up to remind him. A fragment of a song, a whiff of perfume or someone saying something to nudge his thoughts toward her.

"I've missed you, Jessi."

If she let herself, she knew she could become completely unraveled just by the single note of longing in his voice. He'd always been very skillful at making her feel things.

But it wasn't going to happen. Because she wouldn't allow it.

"More like you missed the boat," she corrected crisply. She pushed the remaining piece of salmon about on her plate with her fork for a moment, then raised her eyes to his. "But it's sailed, and it's not coming back to the harbor. Ever," she emphasized. "You and I had something, or so I thought—"

Something twisted inside him to hear her talk like this. "Jessi—"

But she was determined to get this out once and for all and get it over with. He owed her the right to say the words and feel some sort of closure.

"Let me finish, Logan, and then we're not going to talk about this again. You and I had something, but it's gone now."

And not for the world would she allow herself to be put in a position where it returned. Where she vaguely entertained the thought, the hope that it might work between them. Because she already had her answer to that speculation. It wouldn't. Logan Buchanan wasn't the marrying kind. Whether knowingly or unknowingly, what he was was the hurting kind.

Logan didn't believe her. Moreover, he didn't think she believed herself. There was still something electric in the air between them, whether or not either one of them wanted it.

"Is it?" The look in his eyes challenged her. "Is it really gone?"

She met his look and didn't back down. "Yes. I'm a completely different person from the one you knew."

It hadn't been easy, reinventing herself. Taking the best parts and forming the rest until she felt confident that what she'd produced was a stronger version of herself. A version who couldn't be hurt again. She supposed that being here with him, working so close, would be the ultimate test.

Reaching out to her, Logan indulged himself and toyed with the gold hoop at her ear. The slightest touch sent it swaying rhythmically. He watched the candlelight gleam off its rim.

"Not so completely." His voice was a seductive whisper. "You still knock me for a loop every time I look at you."

Nope, not buying. Not even renting, she told herself firmly. "Then my suggestion to you is don't look." Jessica drew her head back, away from his reach. There was such a thing as taking on too much of a challenge. She wasn't about to let herself get singed. "Maybe you'd better get someone else for the job—"

He remembered long, sultry nights where they seemed to make love for hours. He remembered the taste of her mouth and how good the sound of her laughter made him feel. He remembered the good things, because there hadn't been any bad. Except that he'd felt he was in danger of losing himself in her.

"But I want *you*."

The words waltzed along her skin, a haunting refrain from the past visiting the present. She had to deliberately focus on not clenching her hands in her lap as she steeled herself. Why was he doing this? To see how close he could get to breaking her down again?

Resolve galvanized her. "All right, then we do it by my rules." She was issuing a warning. "And you'll cooperate."

Amusement played along his mouth. Logan raised a hand, but gave up the idea of looking solemn. He knew he couldn't pull it off.

"Completely."

The hell he would, Jessica thought. He still thought he could get to her. Well, maybe he could, but it was something Logan wasn't about to ever find out. Not from her.

"And you'll eighty-six any ideas about seducing me," she said pointedly.

He could tease, but he was not in the habit of telling lies. Except the night he'd broken it off with her.

"Now that's going to be a little harder to promise."

"You either promise—and mean it," she warned when he opened his mouth to reply, "or I walk."

She wouldn't. He'd bet his life on it. Jessica was nothing if not loyal to the people she cared about. And she'd cared about him once. She wouldn't just leave him to take this on by himself.

"And leave me to the mercy of poison pens—or printers as it were?"

Whether it was a defense mechanism that made him so flippant, or that the truth of the matter just wouldn't penetrate his thick head, Jessica didn't know. But she didn't care for his attitude.

She sighed, letting her fork drop. This wasn't going to work between them, not if he didn't act seriously. And not if he tried to get under her skin. As well as under a few other things, too.

"It's not a joke, Logan, and I think you realize that. Now I can recommend several very good men—"

"I was never interested in a good man."

"As I recall, you were never interested in a good woman, either," Jessica countered. "You wanted a wanton one."

"*You* weren't," he pointed out.

No, she hadn't been. Not when she met him. But Jessica knew he'd made her want to be. He'd made her want to be anything he wanted, anything he needed. She'd been that in love with him.

Talk about love being blind. "At the time, I thought I was the exception."

"You were."

The room felt as if it was getting smaller. And he was getting closer. She shifted in her seat. "You're doing it again."

What would she do if he kissed her now? Logan wondered. If he rounded the table and just swept her into his arms the way his body was begging him to?

"Doing what?"

She held her ground, though it felt as if it was breaking up beneath her feet. "Going over old times again."

He reached for her hand, curling his fingers around hers. This time she didn't pull back. "I wouldn't have to if I knew there were new times ahead."

The warmth of his skin touching hers seeped in through her. "You're going to make this impossible for me, aren't you?"

He brought her hand to his lips and kissed it lightly. "No, but hopefully memorable."

Jessica could feel the tiny rockets of pleasure shooting off through her system. She struggled not to let them penetrate.

Just then she heard someone coming into the room. Light spilled in from the door as Maxine entered, commandeering the room and saving Jessica from a fatal slip.

Smiling broadly, the cook placed the tray she was carrying on the table beside Jessica. It held two masterpieces of chocolate, whipped cream, almonds and cherries.

"Miss Jessica, you are here, just as Mr. Logan said

you would be." Pleasure resounded in the heavily accented voice. "Is good to see you. How have you been?" Without waiting for an answer, Maxine seldom waited for answers, she looked at Logan. A touch of accusation creased her brow. "She is skinny, not eating my food, yes?"

Jessica could see where the conversation was heading and threw up a barricade quickly. "I was never a big eater, Maxine, but there's nothing I love more than your cooking."

Compliments were her due. Maxine required them, but accepted them as if they were a given.

"This I know, yes. I have dessert," she declared needlessly. "You will eat, yes?"

Amusement filled Jessica. Never having been privy to it, she admittedly adored sporadic mothering. "I will eat, yes."

The look on Maxine's face was solemn, triumphant. "Good." She cleared away the two dinner plates. "Is about time you come back."

Her stamp of approval hung in the air as she retreated through the doorway, taking the light with her. The door closed behind her.

The stifled laugh echoed in Jessica's throat. "She's as charming as ever," she commented, sinking a spoon into Maxine's creation.

As near she could make out, it was some sort of cake, dressed in three kinds of chocolate. Her downfall, she thought. She'd always had no resistance where chocolate was concerned.

Logan laughed. "You're the only one who's ever

said that about Maxine. She usually intimidates people, Dad and Dane included.''

In Jessica's opinion the woman had a heart of gold, but she was nothing if not overbearing and was definitely set in her ways. Jessica looked at Logan thoughtfully. It was to his credit that he overlooked Maxine's flaws and saw only the good.

He'd always had his admirable points. She couldn't have loved him if he hadn't. ''Someone else would have fired her long ago.''

The shrug was careless, as if the intended compliment didn't matter. But it did.

''Someone else doesn't appreciate how hard it is to get a cook who can do the things Maxine does in the kitchen.''

For a moment he paused, watching the look of enjoyment on Jessica's face as she ate. It triggered memories. And desires. Everything about her did.

He searched for the thread of his thought. ''I figure it's worth the minor inconvenience. Besides, everyone's a little eccentric. Look at you.''

She raised her eyes to his. It was the last thing she'd expected him to say. ''Me?''

Logan nodded. He'd think it would be obvious. ''Your parents have all that money and there you are, playing detective—''

She took offense at the word. Being female from a wealthy background, it had taken her a long time to convince people her vocation wasn't a game. ''I'm not playing.''

He saw the momentary flare of annoyance in her

eyes. She'd always been magnificent when angry, though the times had been few and far between. And never at him.

"Sorry, bad choice of words." The apology was genuine. "I meant no disrespect. But it's still eccentric. There you are, risking that pretty neck of yours when you could just be sitting back on some white sand beach while cabana boys fall all over themselves trying to bring you the next fruity, umbrellaed drink, and a squadron of suitors duel for the privilege of having you smile at them."

He certainly painted an elaborate picture, one Jessica knew her mother would have wished she was part of. One she had never remotely indulged in. She had no desire to be pandered to. It was one of the reasons she liked Maxine so well. Maxine never pandered.

Jessica waited until the last forkful had slid all the way down her throat before saying, "You certainly do let yourself get carried away."

"Sometimes," he allowed, then his eyes washed over her significantly. "But not often enough and not when it matters."

The enigmatic remark begged for exploration, but she refused to touch it. There'd be no more talk about them, or the past.

Instead, as they finished their dessert and then drank the exclusive brew that Maxine had concocted within her kitchen that was half coffee, half heaven, Jessica plied Logan with question after question about the board members. She thought that if she approached the subject from every possible angle, he

might remember something that, even in a remote
way, could shed some light on whoever would be
desperate enough to actually resort to threats and vio-
lence.

She could have spared her breath.

Forty-five minutes later, Jessica knew little more
beyond their names and their hobbies. There was no
one who could remember facts better than Logan
when he wanted to, but apparently in this case he
couldn't or wouldn't reveal anything.

With a sigh, Jessica retired her third cup of *Café
Maxine,* as the cook had dubbed the drink, and withdrew from the questioning. Dane would have probably been far more insightful, but Dane wasn't there.
And Logan was.

Logan read her expression correctly as he rose to
his feet.

"Sorry to disappoint you, Jess." Coming around
to stand behind her chair, he helped ease it back as
she stood up. "But for the most part, they're not the
kind of people I usually socialize with. I don't know
all that much about them." He indicated the terrace.
"I think it's not going to rain anymore tonight. Care
for a breath of fresh air?"

The terrace, like everything else in his house, held
too many memories for her. He'd kissed her for the
first time when they were standing on the terrace.
Avoiding it right about now seemed wise.

She shook her head. "I think I should be getting
home."

But as she turned away, he took her hand, forcing her to turn back. He pressed her hand to his chest, the way he did when they danced. She could feel his heart and told herself she didn't care.

"Don't leave yet, Jessi. Stay awhile."

Temptation whispered in her ear like a seductive call. Desperate times called for desperate measures. She resorted to a lie. It felt heavy on her tongue.

"I've got other cases pending, Logan."

He wasn't going to give up that easily. "Can't you give them to your partner?"

She looked at him. Where had he gotten that idea? "I don't have a partner."

"What about that guy in your office? The one who looks like Icabod Crane? Tall, doesn't cast a shadow when he walks," he added for good measure. "Isn't he your partner?"

She wondered how Albert would respond to that idea. He seemed completely content just to be what he was. A right hand she couldn't do without.

"Albert is my assistant, not my partner." She backed up. "And how do you know about Albert, anyway?" According to Albert, they'd never met, and she knew she hadn't mentioned him to Logan.

His expression was inscrutable. "You're not the only one who can do a little digging, a little investigating, you know."

He still thought it was a game for her, didn't he? "I do it for a living."

"I do it to satisfy curiosity."

The words sprang out at her. That was all she was

to him, she thought. And all she'd ever be. A curiosity. An amusement. If she knew that, why was it so hard for her to get it through her thick head?

She didn't like the answer she came up with. Because some part of her still had strong feelings for him.

She didn't care for his methods. Jessica didn't want anyone snooping around in her life, especially not Logan. "If you have any questions about me or my life, ask me."

"All right," he said gamely. "Why won't you stay awhile longer?"

An annoyed hiss escaped through her teeth. "I already told you."

"The truth Jessi."

Her patience was wearing thin. "The truth is that we've already had this dance and moved on." She tried to remember where he'd put her purse. Probably with her coat in the foyer. "When's Dane due back?"

He walked quickly to keep up with her. Jessica could move fast when she wanted to. "Tomorrow."

Taking her coat off the rack, she shoved her arms through the sleeves, putting the raincoat on before he had a chance to hold it for her. The less physical contact, the better.

"Fine. I'll be in touch tomorrow."

In a smooth movement he caught her lapels between his fingers and thumb. Slowly he rubbed his thumbs up and down the material in a motion that could only be called sensual. "Does the condemned man get to kiss you goodbye?"

She wanted to. God help her, despite all the reasons not to, she wanted to let him. But she'd gone that route with him and knew exactly where it led. Knew all the pitfalls to avoid. At the top of the list was allowing him to kiss her.

"No." With a decisive movement, she dropped the straps of her purse on her shoulder. "Tell Maxine the dinner and dessert were wonderful." Turning on her heel, she reached for the door.

"Jessi?"

Jessica bit her lip, holding her breath as she turned only enough to look at him over her shoulder. "What?"

"It was good seeing you again." He'd never meant anything more in his life.

"Uh-huh."

She couldn't leave fast enough.

The next morning she was ten minutes late getting to work. Even that small lapse of time wasn't like her. Clocks could be set by her punctuality.

Albert looked up from his desk. "You look like hell."

She felt like it, too, she thought as she walked by his desk to get to her office. Sleep was something that she had managed to get in five- and ten-minute snatches in between staring at the ceiling and thinking about Logan. It hadn't been a good night.

"Nice to see you, too, Albert," she muttered sarcastically.

He cocked his head, watching her. "Pull an all-nighter?"

Standing before her door, she sighed and turned around. He'd be at her all day unless she set him straight. "Not that it's any business of yours, but I had dinner at the Buchanan house and then I went home." She saw the next question forming. "Early." Jessica pointed toward his computer. "What have you got for me?"

He crossed his arms before his shallow chest. "Other than sage advice?"

She rolled her eyes toward the ceiling, indicating her impatience. "Other than sage advice."

He'd been at it since she gave him the list. "Does the word *zilch* conjure up any images?"

She frowned, walking back to his desk as if that could magically produce some positive results. "None that I want."

"Then sorry to disappoint, but that's the operative word for this morning." He waved a hand at the list on his desk. "Preliminary findings so far show that all these lovely people appear to be solvent and rolling in enough money and stock options to validly sport a label that declares them obscene. I don't think there's a murderer lurking amid them." He paused, thinking of Logan. "But one can always hope."

Logan wasn't all bad. Just bad for her. "You don't mean that."

Albert's chin met his chest as he looked down at her. "Try me."

She didn't need anyone fighting her battles for her.

Or taking offense on her behalf. Not now, at least. "Albert, you really should get a life of your own." She patted his cheek before walking into her own office.

Albert followed her into her office. "Your mother called. Something about your coming to her bachelorette party."

Jessica sang down on her chair with a thud. "Oh, God, she's getting married again."

A nod from Albert confirmed it. "So she said."

What did this make, number four, or was it five? Five, Jessica remembered, if she counted Douglas, whom her mother married twice, squeezing in Antonio in between. She hardly remembered what either man looked like. Her mother would probably say the same thing.

Jessica turned her chair to face Albert. "Did she leave a number where I could reach her?"

He pointed. "On your desk."

She picked up the little blue Post-it. Precise numbers were written in the middle. "What kind of area code is this?"

"Paris, I believe," he recalled. "She said if you took the Concorde immediately, you could be there in time for the party." She pushed the number aside. "You're not going?" he asked, feigning surprise.

"There'll be another in a year or so. There always is." It would be nice to believe that her mother had finally found the right man. She supposed there was always hope. She picked up the other phone message he'd taken for her. "What's this one?"

Straightening, Albert's bearing changed completely. "A woman calling to find out if you took kidnapping cases. Someone abducted her daughter from a mall, and she doesn't feel the police are doing enough."

"They're probably not," Jessica agreed. "Through no fault of their own." She knew a few policemen, detectives who worked homicide. Overworked, every one of them. She opened her drawer, looking for her address book.

Without a word, Albert walked over to her desk, opened another drawer and took out the address book. He placed it in front of her.

"I assume you're looking for this. Although if you ask me, you should refer Buchanan's case to someone else and take this one."

"I didn't ask." She didn't bother telling him that she'd already suggested it and was shot down.

She glanced toward Albert. "But I will ask you to get back to the list of names and keep working with it. Gut feeling says we're missing something."

Jessica turned to the page where she had jotted down the number of ChildFinders, Inc., a local detective agency whose investigators specialized in finding missing children and runaways. Pressing the page down so that she could read it more easily, she dialed the number on the blue slip of paper.

Listening to Savannah King on the other end of the line tell her about the moment her world froze, the moment she realized that her child had been abducted, brought tears to Jessica's eyes.

For a moment she silently fought a battle with herself, wanting to offer her services to the woman in any capacity. But she couldn't be everywhere, couldn't spread herself so thin that she was of no use to anyone. And this woman was better off going to ChildFinders, Inc. The man who ran the agency, Cade Townsend, had experienced the same set of circumstances that the woman found herself in. He would know what to do and how to handle not only the situation, but the woman as well.

The best thing she could do for Savannah King was give her ChildFinders, Inc.'s number. Interrupting her as gently as she could, Jessica told her about the agency and recited the telephone number to her amid assurances that if anyone could help, they could.

That done, Jessica pressed the flash button on the telephone cradle, breaking the connection. Next on her list of phone calls was Alan Burke, who headed Kellogg Labs, an analytical laboratory that specialized in running forensic tests for both the police force and for private investigators. Without a doubt, they were the best in their field. Now that she'd definitely decided to take the case, it was time to go into high gear.

But before she could press the appropriate numbers on the keypad, the telephone rang beneath her outstretched hand, sending a tingling sensation clear through her fingertips.

Maybe it was a sixth sense, or maybe it was because she'd spent the past eight hours thinking about him, but a second before she said a word, Jessica knew the caller was Logan.

"Jessi?"

The sound of his voice saying her name enveloped her like a warm, comforting embrace. Shaking it off, she chalked it up to the vulnerable state she was in after her conversation with Savannah.

But unless she was mistaken, there was also a slight, almost imperceptible edge to his voice. "Logan, what's wrong?"

Chapter 6

He paused before speaking, as if to collect himself and restrict any outward signs that might suggest any image of himself other than the one he wanted her to see. "Does something have to be wrong for me to call my private investigator?"

She knew him too well to be put off the scent by that. Or to retreat. "Why *are* you calling me, Logan? What happened?"

He laughed, but there was a trace of admiration when he spoke. "You didn't tell me a crystal ball was part of your office equipment."

She had no time for cute repartee. "Logan—"

He heard the warning note in her voice and became as serious as he could allow himself to be in the given situation. He had no intention of allowing the threats to actually get to him, or undermine his confidence.

He'd seen what happened to racers when they let doubts creep in. They became a danger to themselves as well as to everyone else. Some creep was trying to do that to him, and he wouldn't allow it.

"Dane thought it might be a good idea if I called and told you that another one of those letters turned up. It arrived in today's mail. Fresh off the mail cart," he added cheerfully.

His chipper voice grated on Jessica's nerves. What did it take for the man to realize how serious this could be? His life was being threatened, and there was always a chance...

Jessica passed her hand over her forehead, unconsciously massaging away the headache that had begun to set up lodging. His words replayed themselves in her head.

"When did Dane get back?"

Maybe she could finally get together with Dane and get something substantial to go on. At the very least, he would know the board members better than Logan apparently did.

"This morning. Went straight to the office, the little workaholic." Dane really had to get himself a life that went beyond spreadsheets and stock options, Logan thought. His brother's brief marriage had lasted less than two years, ending because he'd spent so much time behind one desk or another, flying from one branch office to the next. "Actually, he saw the letter before I did." Logan paused. "Whoever's writing them has stepped up their schedule."

Jessica read between the lines. So, it did bother

him. Maybe, behind the brash words and swaggering attitude, he *was* worried. Jessica felt sympathy twine itself with concern before she locked the emotions away.

"Are you at the office right now?"

"Yes."

Writing quickly, she made a few notes to herself. Maybe she could corral both brothers at once. "Don't go anywhere, I'll be right there."

He had a mental image of Jessica, barefoot on the beach as twilight softly descended. Hurrying toward him. Logan felt his body respond as the memory lingered. "I feel safer already."

She didn't know whether to make him privy to the few choice words that rose to her lips, or just shrug off his response as nerves on his part. If it was the latter, it was a first. Nothing made Logan nervous.

Unless it was commitment.

"Good." She let the receiver drop into the cradle and reached for her purse. So much for getting organized this morning.

"By the way," Albert called into the office after he saw the red light on the telephone go out, "did you see yesterday's paper?"

The days when she'd curl up with the morning paper and a large cup of exotic-tasting coffee were long in her past. "Only as I walked by it on my way out."

"Your fair-haired boys made the news." Albert walked into her office with the section in question held out in his hand. "Specifically, the front page of the business section."

Albert folded the section so that the lead photo sprang up at her. Crossing to her, he dropped the section on her desk. Across the top was the heading "Buchanan brothers take opposite sides in proposed merger."

Jessica picked up the newspaper. Damn. So it was public knowledge now. That was probably what had caused whoever was making the threats to send this latest letter. He undoubtedly assumed that Logan was ignoring him. Not much of a leap.

Eyes skimming down the column, she gave the article a quick, cursory read. Words jumped out at her, just as she knew they would at the person responsible for sending Logan's letters. Specifically the surprising turn taken by someone the news media considered a "globe-trotting, fun-at-any-price personality."

"Terrific." She tossed the paper aside. It slid off her desk. "Damn reporters, anyway."

"My sentiments exactly." Picking up the section, Albert neatly refolded it and placed it on the side of her desk.

The words *damage control* sprang to her mind. This was going to need a lot of it. Jessica glanced at her watch. She had to get rolling. There was no telling how long Logan was going to stay put, and Buchanan Technology was almost twenty miles away. Any morning traffic would just cut into her time.

She glanced at the Post-it note on her desk. She'd forgotten about her mother. "Call my mother, tell her I'm sorry, but I can't make it."

"She's not going to be happy."

So what else was new? "She never is with me. Find out where she's staying and send her three dozen roses...."

She would place the call herself, but she knew there would be an argument if she did. An argument that would end with her mother calling her an ungrateful child for not dutifully turning up at her side to smile for the photographers. There was nothing to be gained by either one of them being agitated. This was better.

Albert's half smile made him look as if he'd just licked a lemon slice. "With or without bougainvillea stems?"

"Without." She pushed the letters on the desk toward him. "And take the letters and that card that came yesterday to Kellogg Labs. While you're at it, you might as well take the box, too. See what Alan can come up with."

Albert nodded, gathering the evidence and placing it in a plastic envelope. He raised his wheat-colored eyebrows to fix her with a look. "Shall I organize the mice to make me a dress for the ball?"

He wouldn't be Albert if he didn't complain. "Only if you really want to, Albert. Light blue gets my vote." She was at the door. "I'll call in later."

With a flick of his wrist, he waved her on her way. "Looking forward to it."

One in a million, she thought, shutting the door behind her. And he was all hers.

With a sigh Jessica put the letter back on the desk. She was in Dane's office with Dane and Logan on either side of her. The door was closed to keep anyone else from hearing. Not that word wasn't somehow leaking out, she thought, even as they were discussing the matter. Like water questing for the one tiny hole it could use to flow through, secrets always seemed to find a way to be discovered.

She looked from one brother to the other. Like the masks for tragedy and comedy in the theater, they looked as if they had completely different reactions to the same situation. Dane was worried while Logan was mildly entertained.

Well, he might be entertained, but she certainly wasn't. She shifted her attention to Dane, the sensible one.

"My first thought is that we really should call the police."

Dane looked horrified. "Didn't you read the letter?" He started to jab a finger at the paper, then thought better of it. The fewer prints, the better. "He said no police, or he'll set a bomb off in one of the warehouses or the office building. There's no way we can tell where. If word gets out, the whole merger dies right here."

"Not to mention how many people could get hurt." Logan's mild tone understated the seriousness of the statement.

"Yes, of course." Dane ran a nervous hand over his thinning hair. "That, too." His eyes darted from Logan to Jessica. Ever since the first letter had appeared, he'd been like a man on a journey to an inevitable nervous breakdown. "Jessica, we can't risk calling the police in on this."

"I agree with Dane." Logan folded his arms before him, perching on the edge of Dane's desk with the air of a man who didn't have a care in the world. "No police."

This was beginning to feel bigger than she was. She looked at the letter again.

I warned you. Don't impede the merger or you'll forfeit your life. Call the police and some of your people will forfeit theirs. Bomb, bomb, where's the bomb? The office? The warehouse? You won't have to guess if you talk to the police.

Uneasiness undulated through her. She looked at Logan. "They can take steps to protect you."

It seemed odd, to be comforting her about his death threat. Opportunities came in strange packages. Logan took her hands in his.

"You know and I know that's not true. They can't do anything except help me get a restraining order issued." A smile played on his lips at the irony. "If they knew who was supposed to be restrained. Their hands are tied until someone actually tries to kill me."

A chill swept up her spine. He was right. "Been doing your homework?"

He inclined his head. "Just trying to keep up with you."

She realized he was still holding her hands.

Straightening her shoulders, she pulled away. "This isn't the time to flirt, Logan."

He raised one brow as a smile she once thought she couldn't resist curved his mouth wider. "You'll tell me when, then?"

She didn't know whether to laugh in disbelief, succumb or just hit him. Instead, she chose to hold her ground and her temper. "This is serious, Logan. Will you finally get that through your thick head?"

He rose from the desk, glancing at his brother. Dane looked a little pale. For his sake, Logan sobered. "Consider it 'gotten.'" He looked at her, looked past her angry expression and into her eyes. Into her soul. "We all deal with tension in our own way. Me, I flirt with you."

"Or anything that's breathing." It was an automatic, flippant response, said without thinking. She knew it was beneath her. Jessica held up a hand before he said anything. "Sorry, that's old territory and I'm not going there. You need protection—"

He couldn't resist. "Why, are we going to make love?"

"Logan!" Maybe hitting him was the way to go. With a two-by-four.

He grinned, hands raised as if to defend himself against her if she decided to let loose. He knew he'd crossed the line, but having her angry at him was preferable to having her indifferent to him. Anger was a passionate emotion, and passion was what he ultimately wanted to evoke from her.

"Sorry. I'll try to be serious."

Dane cleared his throat. Jessica looked in his direction. "You're right about the protection."

Finally. "At least someone's making sense here," she said with relief.

Dane fished out his personal checkbook from his breast pocket. "Name your price."

A little of the relief began to fade. "Excuse me?"

Dane pushed down the top of the gold pen his grandfather had given him years earlier. Given to sentiment, he saved pieces of life rather than live them. "I'm assuming that you'll charge extra to be Logan's bodyguard."

Dane had taken one hell of a large leap from point A to point B. Jessica felt herself being backed into a corner and dug her heels in.

"You just stopped making sense, Dane."

Not looking at Logan, Dane pressed on. "Isn't one of your functions to be a bodyguard?"

It wasn't something she did with any frequency, but she had assumed the role two or three times, when the situation warranted it.

"Yes, but—"

"Jessica, there is no 'but' about it." He waved a hand at Logan. "We both know Logan won't stand for a stranger shadowing his every move. You two have a history. He'll let you near him."

Logan only allowed others to speak for him when it served his purpose, but even now he found himself getting annoyed at being treated as if he were part of the furnishings.

He stepped between them. "Sometimes Dane takes

being a big brother too far. But he is right.'' He looked down at Jessica. ''If I have to have a bodyguard around, cramping my style and getting in the way, I'd want it to be you or no one.''

There were more pitfalls for her here than in a fully loaded minefield. She'd be a fool to agree to this. ''Logan—''

''Or no one,'' he repeated quietly.

It was, she knew, an ultimatum. Damn him, anyway. ''I could call your bluff, you know,'' she informed him, unconsciously rising on her toes. ''Just walk out.''

He knew her too well. Or hoped he did. ''You've got too big a heart for that, Jessi.''

In the space of a second, she heaped enough curses on his head to make his blood curl if she'd said them out loud. ''For two cents—''

''It'll be a lot more than two cents—'' Logan promised. Whatever her price, it didn't matter. This was a tremendous opportunity to bring her back into his life, really bring her back. And face his own demons.

He was beginning to think he owed whoever was writing these letters a vote of thanks.

''I don't need the money—''

Logan knew she was partially estranged from her family but had no idea what her current financial state was. Jessica wouldn't let on even if she was hurting for funds. It wasn't her way. ''We'll make the check out to your favorite charity, then.''

The less time she wasted here, arguing with him,

the more she'd have to solve this thing. Besides, she'd managed to survive these last two years, getting over him. What difference could one more week make?

"Fine." She bit off the word, thrusting her hand out toward Dane rather than Logan. "You've got yourself a bodyguard." She glanced toward Logan. "But just until the stockholders' meeting on Saturday."

He couldn't resist teasing her. It was either that, or sweep her into his arms and allow himself to get lost in the scent that was hers exclusively. A scent no manufacturer could come close to duplicating.

"Could we reciprocate once in a while?" His eyes were soft, sensual despite their gleam. "I'll guard your body instead of you guarding mine?" He held up his hand, an innocent Boy Scout taking an oath of allegiance. "I promise to do an excellent job."

"Don't push me too hard, Logan. I'm carrying a gun."

His eyes met hers and held. "Lethal women always did turn me on."

It was going to be the longest four days on record. "You are hopeless, you know that?"

Ignoring Dane, who'd cleared his throat to gain their attention, Logan slipped his hands down along her arms to cup her elbows. The humor in his eyes settled down to a gentle amusement.

"No, Jessi, I am never without hope."

A sinking feeling in the pit of her stomach warned her that she had just bitten off an immense piece that defied consumption. Only inherent stubbornness made

her determined to see this through. She was *not* going
to succumb to a man who could only offer her a one-
way ticket to absolutely nowhere.

Worn heels hit the floor arrythmically as he paced
from corner to corner within the room. Thinking.
Planning. Anticipating.

He wondered how long he should toy with his prey.
He was impatient for the end to come. Impatient for
the cleansing feeling to wash over him, telling him
that he had finally closed that chapter of his life.

Yet anticipation had its rewards. And torture its
thrills.

He wanted to make his prey suffer in all the ways
that he had himself come to suffer.

That required time.

With a magnanimous wave of his thin hand, he
made his decision, awarding his prey a little extra
time. And so, in giving a little, he would have more.

He was already enjoying it.

A squeaking sound escaped his lips, sounding like
a child's giggle. There was no one to hear him in the
apartment.

"You're staying at his house?" Albert's voice was
almost a squeak, coming over her apartment phone.

She doubted he would have sounded more disapproving if she'd said she was moving into a brothel.
Probably less.

Jessica could just visualize his expression. "Wipe
the disapproving look off your face Albert, I can hear

it in your voice.'' Moving between her closet and the open suitcase on her bed, Jessica selected clothes and tossed them in the general vicinity of the valise. ''Logan's getting more threats, and he won't go to the police. Can't, really,'' she amended.

She remembered the look on Logan's face when he pointed out that deaths other than his own would result if he went to the police. He'd actually been concerned. She supposed that there was hope for him yet.

Juggling the phone, she took a white-trimmed navy sheath from the hanger and added it to the small collection near her valise. ''This person we're looking for could very well be desperate enough to try to hurt him.''

''If he can hurt Buchanan, he can hurt you.''

She paused, smiling to herself. He really was more a big brother than an assistant.

''Albert, I'm a private investigator. A little danger goes with the territory. If I wanted to be safe, I would have become a taxidermist.''

''It has its pluses.''

Jessica didn't have time to debate this. She'd promised to return to Logan's office in an hour, after she'd packed and dropped her clothes off. ''I just called to let you know where you can reach me in case the cell phone doesn't pick up your signal, not to argue about this with you. And to find out if you'd come up with anything on your end yet.''

''Turns out one of the ladies on the board of Buchanan Tech ran afoul of the law when she was a teenager. One Cynthia Darrow. Daddy used to be VP at Washington Savings and Loan until that nasty scandal when they went belly-up. Her juvenile records were sealed, thanks to 'Daddy,' when she turned eighteen.''

Finally, something. She knew she could count on Albert. ''You sly dog. Any way to find out what was sealed in them?''

She heard the keyboard clicking as he answered, ''I'm working on it.''

''My hero.'' Receiver propped up against her shoulder and neck, she pulled open her lingerie drawer. ''You've been a great help, Albert.''

''I can be an even greater help if—''

She headed him off before he could start in again. ''Just work the list, Albert.''

''And you make sure he doesn't work you,'' Albert warned sternly. ''Remember the last time.''

''Exactly,'' she answered.

It was a good game plan. She fervently hoped she could stick to it.

Chapter 7

Rules, Jessica silently chanted to herself as she threw her suitcase into the back seat of her car. She needed to remember the rules. The cardinal rule—Never Get Personally Involved with a Client—she'd already splintered and broken. But if she changed the key word to *Reinvolved,* she might still have a chance of making it work.

All she had to do was remember to abide by it.

Bracing herself, Jessica started the car. She felt like someone about to undertake a thousand-mile journey across quicksand with only a narrow strip, set smack in the middle, that was safe ground. How long before she lost her balance and fell in?

Jessica's hands tightened on the steering wheel as she came to a stop at a light. If she felt that way, what the hell was she doing, taking this case?

Because Logan wouldn't have anyone else and his life might actually be in danger, that's what. She didn't want him back in her life, but she certainly didn't want him dead, either.

A rock and a hard place, that was where she was setting up residence. Jessica sighed. She should have packed something more comfortable to wear. Like protective foam rubber. Something told her she was going to be rubbed raw before the case was over.

It didn't take her long to drive to Logan's house. Neil greeted her like an old friend, then opened the gates for her. She watched them dubiously before she drove through. The schematic had assured her that bypassing the system would take a real professional, and scaling the fence was next to impossible. The volts that coursed through them could easily light up the sky on the next Fourth of July celebration for miles to come.

But every puzzle had a solution and every system had its master. She wouldn't feel at ease about Logan's safety until the vote was in on Saturday and the merger settled one way or another.

After that, he was on his own.

Just the way he'd always been, she thought. And always liked it.

Parking the car at the end of the winding gray-and-white-paved driveway, Jessica took out her suitcase and hurried up the steps. She had a little time before she was to meet with Cynthia Darrow, enough to settle in.

She'd called before leaving her apartment. The woman who'd answered Cynthia's phone had been her secretary. She'd been reluctant to agree to a meeting, but Jessica had insisted. Telling her she was acting on Logan's behalf was what had actually gotten her the appointment, though. After mentioning his name, it was as if doors opened and seas parted.

He'd always had that effect on women, she mused, pressing the doorbell. All women.

She was surprised to see Logan standing there when the door opened. She thought she'd left him at his office. Jessica rallied quickly enough.

"What are you doing here?"

He stepped back, holding the door for her. "I live here, remember?"

He'd opted for being charming again. Mentally, she adjusted her armor and went on the attack. It was easier to deal with him when she was annoyed. "Did you have to release that story to the newspaper?"

His hand slipped over hers and he took the suitcase from her. It felt light. Wasn't she staying until the end of the week? "This all you're bringing?"

"Aside from the laptop." For the time being, she'd left it in her trunk. "I travel light."

He led the way into the foyer. Memories echoed through his mind…were they really only two years old? "I can remember a time when all you needed to pack were your vitamins."

She swung around to face him. "And I can remember a time when I believed in fairy tales. All part of the past, Logan. And you're changing the subject.

Why did you have to give the interview on the merger? That's like poking a stick into the hole of an active beehive.''

So, she still didn't understand that he'd changed since his father's death, he thought. Why should she? The change had come after they'd stopped seeing each other.

''I didn't 'have to,' it was just another way to make my stand a little more public. I'm serious about this, Jess, and I want to get to as many people as possible about putting a stop to the merger.''

Exasperation overtook her. He was smarter than that. The last thing he needed in his situation was to attract publicity for his so-called ''stand.''

''Well, there's your answer why you got another poison pen letter from your pen pal so quickly. Damn it, Logan, he means business.''

What did she have to do to make him appreciate that fact? Who knew what the person they were dealing with was capable of? Maybe he had a flagrant disregard of life, as long as it meant winning.

''And I'm *in* business,'' Logan said just as emphatically. He looked at her, struggling with his own anger. Anger because he had to watch his back because some degenerate with a printer was sending him empty threats. ''I won't be cornered, Jessica.''

The laugh was dry, but not without feeling. ''I, above all people know that, Logan. But a little discretion when you're being threatened would be nice.'' She glanced up toward the stairs, wondering which room would be hers. And if it had a lock on it.

He shrugged carelessly. All water under the bridge. "Dane and I gave the okay for the story before this turned out to be a major issue." Anger at his own impotence took hold. A man should be able to look out for himself. "What would you have suggested I do? Back down? Say 'Sorry, someone's sending me nasty notes so I can't talk to you about the company my grandfather put together'? A company standing at its first crossroads in twenty years?" He shook his head. "Not my style, Jessi."

She knew all about his style and his way. They were what had drawn her in. And then caused the breakup.

"Let's hope you have some style left to speak of, after all this is over." Staring at him, she watched for some sign of recognition as she asked, "What do you know about Cynthia Darrow?"

He thought a moment, raising an image to go with the name. The present image wasn't the one he kept under wraps. "Too many birds on her antenna."

She had no idea how to read him. "Are you being literal or is that a euphemism?"

Once, it might have been the latter, Logan thought. But no more. And that was the pity of it. Cynthia's father, though full of the best intentions, had turned her into exactly what the old man had dreaded.

"She's strange. Not dangerous strange," Logan clarified when he saw the light entering her eyes. "Eccentric strange. Too much medication mixed in with years of mind-numbing therapy." He remembered the stories. For a pocket of time, his father had even gone out with Cynthia. "She was a wild child." Part was hearsay, and part he had gotten firsthand. "She loved to aggravate her father." He glanced at Jessica, wondering how much she could relate to. Her own father had ignored her for the most part, a lot like Cynthia's father had ignored her. But with a world of difference as to the results. "The usual, boring, poor-little-rich-girl thing," he explained, seeing her puzzled expression. "Except that where Cynthia was concerned, she made eradicating boredom an art form."

Jessica wondered if it was her imagination, or if she detected a touch of sadness in Logan's voice as he continued.

"When she ran afoul of the law, her father supposedly greased a lot of palms to make the offense go away. He made her go away, too. Sent her off to some fancy clinic. Dane heard they used shock treatment on her. I don't know that for a fact, except that she does act a little vacant, but then, she was never there a hundred percent to begin with." A smile tugged on his mouth. "When she was younger, she believed in experimenting with whatever recreational drug was out there for the getting. I think she called it 'experiencing' but the bottom line's the same. She was messed up long before she was sent away." And that was the pity of it. It was a waste of what could have been a beautiful human being.

He looked at Jessica, knowing what she was waiting to hear. "But she's harmless enough. Why, do you think she's responsible for the letters?"

Jessica reached for her suitcase again. "Worth a look."

He beat her to it and reclaimed the valise. He wondered what was taking Julia so long. The housekeeper should have been here by now.

"I doubt if Cynthia knows how to operate a computer to get it to print anything." He dismissed the idea as completely absurd. "Not her generation or her calling."

Was he being defensive of the woman? Why? "Well, I have to start somewhere."

He thought it an odd place to begin. Cynthia wouldn't have been his first choice by any means. "You intend to question everyone on the board?"

She had to do something. "That's the plan until a better one comes up."

"What about my body?" He looked at her with an innocence that almost worked. If it hadn't been Logan.

She stared at him. "Excuse me?"

He was tempted to drop the suitcase and just pull her to him. Which was why he continued holding the valise. "Aren't you supposed to guard it? Or have you figured out how to be two places at once?"

These were the times when she sorely missed having a partner, the way Kade did at ChildFinders. Someone to work with her and pick up the slack.

"Not yet. But you can come with me." It was the only viable solution.

"Jessica, I'm shocked." With dramatic flair, he

splayed his hand over his chest. "I'm a working man, I can't just cut out when the whim moves me."

It was all she could do not to laugh in his face. He didn't actually think she'd believe that, did he? "Since when?"

He thought of his life before his father's death. So much wasted time. So many opportunities not taken. He'd hardly known his father until the end. And hadn't really realized how important their company was to the future of space exploration. That was when he'd decided to take an active interest, an active part. It was never too late to make amends.

At least in some cases.

"Since I decided that being on a permanent vacation devalued the experience," he told her.

She tried to read between the lines. Was there more going on? Even at his least complicated, Logan had never been an easy man to understand.

"In other words, you have to do a little work in order to be able to go on vacation?"

Logan grinned. "Something like that." He casually shrugged his shoulders to underscore his point. "Besides, the company does have my name on it. Maybe it should have a little of my sweat in it, too." He saw the incredulous expression come over her face. "What's the matter, Jessi? You look surprised."

"I guess I am."

He thought of the few serious conversations they'd had. The few that he had allowed to take place. For the most part he'd never wanted anything serious to enter into any of the relationships he'd had. Seriousness was the first step to a place he'd never wanted to inhabit. His father's example was one he'd wanted to avoid at all cost. He'd wanted to remain invincible and invulnerable, needing no one but himself.

So what had gone wrong?

"This is what you always wanted me to be like, isn't it?" he asked.

"I never told you what to do."

Jessica never would have presumed to do that. At the time, she'd loved everything about him just the way he was. It was only in the deepest part of her heart that she wished he was a little more serious, a little more dedicated to something other than having a wonderful, carefree time.

"No," he granted, reaching out to run his hand lightly along her face. Her skin still felt soft. And enticing. "But underneath, I knew you thought I was just a wee bit too devil-may-care and rootless to suit that Anglo-Saxon work ethic beating within that gorgeous chest of yours."

She felt herself growing warm. That wasn't part of the job description. "You're digressing."

He looked deep into her eyes and realized he wasn't as afraid as he'd once been. Realized, too, that the adoration he'd seen there once was gone now. He felt the pang of loss. "I only wish I could."

Jessica took a deep breath, but she didn't pull back her head the way she knew she should. She hadn't the strength for anything but a warning. "This isn't going to work if you don't play by the rules."

He feathered his fingers through her hair. "Couldn't we make them up as we go along?"

"Logan..." Her voice was a warning.

His was a whisper that sent currents of longing through her. "Jessica..."

"I'm serious."

He sighed, dropping his hand to his side. Retreating for the time being. "Yes, I know you are. All right, I'll be good."

She laughed, but it was a soft sound. "That'll be the day."

Logan leaned closer to her, though there was no one around to hear. "As I recall, you once thought I was very good."

And then the cavalry arrived, wearing sensible shoes, and a long navy dress to hide legs that Jessica knew were slightly bowed. Julia Maypole smiled at her, transforming a plain, well-lined face into a pretty one.

Greeting her warmly, Julia reached for the suitcase on the floor beside Logan. "Will you be staying in the green room, Miss Jessica?"

Logan shook his head, changing his mind about the arrangements. "No, put Miss Jessica's things in the room next to mine, Julia."

That was far too close for comfort. The first time she'd stayed here, she'd been in the room next to Logan's. For all of ten minutes. After that, she'd stayed in his. "The green room will be fine, Julia."

Julia looked at Logan for confirmation.

He played his only card. "I'm just thinking of the

job, Jessi. Aren't you supposed to stick close to me at all times?''

Suddenly he was worried? That would be the day. ''Down the hall is close enough.''

He nodded to Julia, giving his permission. Then, turning to Jessica, he pretended to sigh. ''So near and yet so far.''

He looked so comical and so damn appealing at the same time, she couldn't help laughing. ''You really are impossible.''

Her reaction pleased him. ''You used to laugh just like that when you said it.''

The recollection surprised her. ''You remember?''

He took her hands into his. ''I remember a lot more than you know.''

And she would be a fool if she believed that. The temptation to be a fool struggled hard to surface. It lost the battle. For now. ''All right, let's get started.''

The chuckle rumbled deep in his chest. ''I thought you'd never ask.''

Hearing him laugh still affected her. She wasn't pleased about it. ''Logan, I mean going to question Cynthia.''

He knew that was what she meant. Resigned, he nodded, then led her to the front door. ''That'll have to wait, unless your meeting's after two.''

She didn't understand. ''Why will it have to wait?''

''Because I have a meeting to get back to.'' He glanced at his watch to confirm the time. He had to be there in less than half an hour. ''They should be back from lunch now.''

Going back to the office in the middle of the day wasn't like him. For that matter, neither was going to the office, period. "Then why did you come back here?"

"I wanted to be here to welcome you. Call me nostalgic."

His smile went straight to her core. The struggle to remain detached continued. "You don't have a nostalgic bone in your body."

He winked at her the way he used to. She experienced the same reaction. Damn, this was going to be difficult, she thought.

"Why don't you examine me later and see?"

She decided to ignore the comment completely. "I'll have to call Cynthia from your car phone."

He laughed, opening the front door for her. "Spoilsport."

When they finally arrived at the Darrow residence, it was closer to six o'clock than not. Logan's meeting had run over, and Jessica had had to leave the meeting at one point to reschedule.

Though less impressive than Logan's estate, the house was still far beyond what the average man could aspire to. She thought of her own modest house and felt almost homesick. The house had a stale scent to it the moment the door was opened to admit them. It smelled of rose water, old dreams and dust.

"You'll make this short, I trust?" the secretary asked, sounding very much like a protective warden.

"As short as we can," Jessica promised.

To her surprise, Logan grinned at the woman. "Hello Rosie, how is she?"

"The same." Only two words, the response was filled with all the warmth that was missing from her voice when she spoke to Jessica.

The man definitely had a way about him, Jessica thought grudgingly as she followed the woman. Jessica made a mental note to ask Logan where he knew Cynthia's secretary from.

The room Cynthia Darrow greeted them in looked like something that belonged in a Victorian novel. A stereotypical one at that. Jessica looked around slowly. It seemed as if every square inch was taken up by knickknacks. Knickknacks that vied for space and absorbed dust that refused to be banished.

Jessica could feel her sinuses protesting the moment she walked in.

"How nice of you to come." Blinking several times like a signal whose gears were stuck, Cynthia looked from Jessica to Logan. "Can you stay long?"

Jessica exchanged looks with Logan. She could see the words *I told you so,* clearly in his eyes.

"Not long, Cynthia," Logan answered. Taking Jessica's arm, he indicated a small, cleared space on the sofa for her to sit. The rest was taken up by stacks of newspapers. Jessica began to feel that she wasn't nearly as bad a housekeeper as she thought.

Rather than compete with the newspapers, Jessica elected to stand. "I just wanted to meet you so I could ask a few questions."

Wariness slipped into her gray eyes. Long, limp

blond hair framed a face that had once been animated
but was now wan. Badly chewed fingernails fluttered
at Cynthia's throat as she pressed her hand there.
"Questions? What kind of questions?" Her voice
picked up speed. "I don't like questions. They pry.
Are you going to pry?"

Either the woman had overdosed on Gloria Swan-
son's portrayal of the faded screen star in the original
version of *Sunset Boulevard,* or she was everything
Logan had said she was. Jessica meant to find out.

"Mr. Buchanan's been getting death threats. We
were wondering if you might have any idea who
would be sending them."

She rolled her gray eyes like marbles at Logan. The
panic expression relaxed. She looked almost coquet-
tish as she smiled at him.

"Death threats? Logan, what have you been up to?
Have you been misbehaving again? Logan can be
very wicked, you know," she confided to Jessica.
"He has quite the reputation."

Now there was an understatement. "Yes, I know."
Since the woman appeared to have calmed down, Jessica decided to press a little. "If you could just stop
to think for a second—"

"Think? Oh, but I don't want to think." Picking
up speed again, Cynthia's voice galloped from one
word to the next, an untamed mustang looking for the
one crack in the fencing. "It hurts my head too much
to think. Maybe later. Yes, later. Later, I'll think. Will
that be all right? Would you like to see my collection?" she went on without waiting for an answer and

obviously losing the thread of her thought. Eagerly she reached for one of the numerous figurines on the massive hutch that stood behind her.

Logan crossed to her. "No, that's all right, Cynthia," he said gently. "We'll have to take a rain check for now."

Her eyes widened. She looked toward the window, staring as if she could see through the drawn draperies. "Rain check? Is it raining? Oh, dear, then I'll get wet if I go out. I shouldn't go out."

Well, this wasn't going anywhere, Jessica thought. She took the woman's hand in hers, directing Cynthia's attention toward her. "Thank you very much for your time."

Cynthia nodded vigorously. "Bye, come again when it isn't raining." Forgetting them the moment she turned away, she busied herself with her figurines.

Jessica waited until they had walked out the front door and were out of the secretary's earshot. The woman had materialized the moment they left Cynthia's room. "This woman is on the board of directors?"

"It's her father's seat. She has it out of the company's respect for him."

"Does she actually come to vote?"

He opened the car door for her, then shut it when she got in. "Her lawyer handles the vote."

Jessica buckled up. "Then maybe we should be seeing him."

Logan followed suit, then turned on the ignition.

The Jaguar roared to life. "He's out of the country right now."

She looked at him thoughtfully. Why hadn't he said any of this before they'd left to see Cynthia? "You seem to know an awful lot about her."

He passed it off lightly. "You pick up things." And then he smiled. He'd let this go on far enough. "Besides, I have a soft spot in my heart for her."

She'd been aware of that the moment they had walked into Cynthia's parlor. "Why?"

He turned out of the estate. Faced with a fork in the road, he made his choice. They went right. "You don't want to know."

She told herself her curiosity only had to do with the case. "Maybe I do."

He paused, then went ahead. She'd asked for it. "She was my first."

The admission rendered Jessica momentarily speechless. "You seduced her?"

Logan laughed. "The other way around. Cynthia seduced me."

She couldn't picture Logan with the eccentric, disoriented woman they'd just left. "She's twenty years older than you."

"Ten," he corrected. "She just looks twenty years older. And she wasn't always the way she is now." His smile was tender, his memories more so. "At twenty-four she was really something else."

"Twenty-four?" Jessica echoed. "That would have made you—"

He knew exactly how old he'd been. And how truly grateful for the initiation rite.

"I was just fifteen. It was my birthday." And Cynthia had called it a birthday present. Both their fathers would have gone into shock if they'd discovered them. But hers had been away in Japan and his had been pleasantly drunk somewhere, beyond caring. "I don't think Cynthia's the one who's responsible for the death threats, Jessi."

Obviously. Jessica settled back in the seat, feeling far from calm. "Then why'd you come along?"

"I didn't want to argue with you about her. I thought you had to see her for yourself to understand."

But there was still something bothering her. "Albert says her finances aren't as good as they might appear." And it took money to run that house. The taxes alone had to be monumental.

"I know," he said matter-of-factly. "She fell on hard times when her father died. I got her the lawyer and made some arrangements."

"Arrangements?" she pressed.

He sighed. She wouldn't be happy until he told her all of it. "I set aside some money to take care of her. Just a small trust fund."

She'd never thought of him as a Good Samaritan. "You?"

He glanced at her as he took a turn. "Don't look so surprised, Jess. Once in a while, even Satan can do a good deed."

"I never thought you were Satan."

She thought of him as a hell of a lot worse than that and he knew it, Logan thought.

"You're insulting my intelligence. Enough investigating for one day," he told her. "I think dinner is in order. I know this little club—"

He was taking charge again. After what she'd just discovered, she had to admit she was inclined to let him. At least for the moment. "Do I have any say in this matter?"

"No."

She settled back again. "All right, then let's go."

"Knew you'd see things my way, given time." He pressed down on the accelerator.

That was just the problem, she thought. She could always see things his way.

Chapter 8

The thin, tuxedoed waiter looked to be around thirty and seemed to possess no hips to speak of. He looked patiently at Logan. "May I take your order now?"

"Yes." Logan closed his menu, placing it on the table. The candle in the round, rose-colored bowl flickered. This had been one of their favorite restaurants when they'd been together, and he'd brought her here in hopes of stirring up old memories. "The lady will have—"

Jessica raised an eyebrow. "The lady hasn't made up her mind yet."

"The lady hasn't made up her mind yet," Logan echoed with a smile. Looked like he'd overstepped himself again, he thought. "We'll need a little more time." He waited until the waiter withdrew before leaning over to Jessica. "The menu's basically the same as when we used to come here."

She'd lowered her eyes again and resumed perusing the menu. Nothing tempted her appetite. Thanks to her nerves, no doubt.

"But I'm not."

He laughed out loud, catching her attention. "Feisty and independent. I like that."

Maybe, maybe not, she mused. "We'll see."

"Yes." He smiled. "We will." Logan took a long sip from his drink, then set it down again.

Settling on a Caesar salad, she looked at the glass he'd just put down. "I don't recall ever seeing you drink ginger ale before." When they had been together, he'd favored scotch and sodas, and meals were always accompanied by glasses of vintage wines.

Ginger ale was a habit he'd made himself acquire. Logan raised the glass, holding it to the light as if to examine what he already knew to be true.

"The color's right to keep people from asking questions." This was a drastic change from his partying days. He set the glass aside. He'd much rather look at her. "I find myself wanting a good, strong drink occasionally, but for the most part, this'll do."

Jessica couldn't help being surprised. "Why the change?" She saw the faraway look in his eyes. "Was it your father?"

He didn't really want to get into that tonight. It was far too serious a topic to discuss when seduction was on his mind.

"You do like playing detective, don't you?"

He hadn't said it to demean her, only to deter her, so she took no offense.

"Being, not playing," Jessica corrected.

"As you wish," he allowed indulgently. If pressed, he would have said he really didn't like the idea of Jessica being a private investigator, but he'd lost the right to have any say in her life. "And yes, it's because by the time dear old dad was my age, the doctor said his liver was more pickled than anything you could find in the condiment section of your friendly neighborhood supermarket."

And he was determined not to follow in his father's footsteps. It was an admirable notion, except that his father's example, she knew now, was also what kept Logan from ever getting serious with a woman. Because his father had become serious with *every* woman. And had his heart broken by each one.

"But you feel free to go right ahead and order something stronger for yourself," he said, pointing at her drink. When the waiter had taken their order for cocktails, Jessica had echoed his choice. He remembered that she usually consumed colorful concoctions served in tall, frosty glasses with thin straws. His smile unfurled like warm vapor along the moors. "As a matter of fact, I insist on it."

Jessica toyed with her straw, poking at the cherry she'd requested. It bobbed elusively in the amber liquid. "Trying to ply me with liquor to get me drunk so you can have your way with me?"

Logan snapped his fingers and sighed heavily. "Damn, am I that obvious?"

She laughed at his performance. "Only when you want to be. Ginger ale's fine with me." As far as she was concerned, she was on duty. "I like having my senses sharp, not dull."

He studied her for a long moment, playing with the words in his mind. He set them free. "That's how I felt when we made love. You were far headier than any alcoholic drink I ever had."

The comment warmed her and she knew she was swiftly headed for very dangerous ground. She stopped toying with her straw and looked at him seriously. "Let's make a truce. I won't upbraid you for the past if you don't bring it up."

Had she successfully hardened herself to him? Or was the opposite true. Was he getting to her? Was she trying to keep him from gaining ground? The thrill of the game filled him.

"Any of it?" he wanted to know.

Her eyes met his. She meant business. "Any of it."

Had she stopped caring the moment they'd broken up, or had it taken her time to get over him? Over them? He wanted to know because seeing her had convinced him that he'd never gotten over her. Not really.

"There were some good moments, weren't there, Jessi?"

If she didn't know better, she would have sworn that there was a genuinely tender note in his voice. And that he wanted to go back to that time in their life. If he did, it was only to bed her again. They'd been good together in bed. Very good. It was only when they were out of bed that the problems began.

"There were a lot of good moments, Logan, but I don't want to go over them." Assignment or not, maybe she *should* have gotten something stronger to drink, she thought. Just a little to fortify her against him and harden her resolve.

She doubted if there was that much alcohol available in the world.

"Why?" Covering her hand with his own, he stroked it lightly with his thumb. "Afraid you might want to relive it?"

Shock waves raced up and down her arm, spreading from there.

"No," she lied, and fought to keep a steady gaze. "I'm not afraid. And I don't want to relive anything." Withdrawing her hand, she picked up her glass. "Been there, done that. Besides, I like me a lot better with a backbone."

Her self-image didn't jibe with what he knew of her. "You *always* had a backbone, Jess. The way you stood up to your parents would have made James Dean proud." He toasted her with his ginger ale. "Rebel *with* a cause, that was you."

He was right, but she was surprised that he'd noticed that about her. It was only around him that her backbone seemed to dissolve.

He raised his eyes from her face, looking behind her. Making eye contact, he nodded. "I think our waiter's hovering again. Made up your mind, yet?"

She looked at him. "Absolutely," she declared firmly. *I think.*

She felt strange returning to Logan's house after dinner, knowing that nothing would follow. That she would go to her room and he to his until daylight made its appearance again. Strange and oddly lonely, even though this was exactly what she wanted. Getting involved with Logan, any more than she already was, would only be allowing herself to retrace steps she'd already taken once. A summer rerun.

She wanted the impossible. A first-run feature.

When they walked in, Julia informed them that "Mr. Dane" had taken the red-eye to San Diego, then, with no further instructions to follow, she withdrew for the night. Maxine, she'd added as she left, had already gone to bed an hour ago.

They might as well have been alone in the house. Life, Jessica thought, was made up of many tests. This was one of hers.

He brought her to her door, then lingered. She wondered if he was trying to see if he could talk his way into her room. She was determined not to succumb, and clung to her shredding work ethic as if it were a life preserver.

The window at the end of the hall was open, stirring the warm spring air. Bringing her fragrance to him. He figured it went under the heading of cruel and unusual punishment.

He could feel himself getting aroused.

Indulging himself, Logan toyed with a wisp of hair at the nape of her neck.

"Well, one day down, four more to go. Think you can put up with me for that long, Jessi?"

It was only because she'd stiffened her shoulders that she'd successfully squelched the shiver that wanted to shimmy down her spine, taking possession.

"I'll manage."

A smile teased his lips. "I'm not sure I can, knowing you're just half a hallway away."

"*You'll* manage," she assured him. And just in case he couldn't, she intended to use the lock on her door to keep him out...and herself in.

"You do know where to find me if you need something?"

He didn't want to "manage." But he didn't want to force himself on her, either. There was no satisfaction in that.

Whether or not she needed something was her own problem, not his. "Just as long as it's not at my door," she told him.

She knew him better than that, he told himself. She knew he wouldn't push.

Just coax.

He skimmed his fingertip along the outline of her throat. She pulled her head back, but he'd seen her pulse jump. "Aren't you afraid someone might shoot me in your sleep?"

She smiled at his choice of words. "If that happens, I'll just have to refund your brother's money."

"You could avoid that problem if you just stayed

in my room for the night. Or let me sleep in yours.''
His innocent expression clashed with the wicked look
in his eyes.

''And find a whole new set of problems? No, thank
you.'' Though she smiled, her answer was firm and
nonnegotiable. ''We're supposed to do it my way,
remember?''

Hand on the wall above her head, Logan leaned in
closer to her, cutting off her air supply. His face was
only a few inches from hers.

''Nothing I can do to change your mind about the
sleeping arrangements?''

Her smile froze in place. Her eyes were steely.
''Nothing.''

Denied access at the gate, he tried another avenue
of approach. ''Then is the condemned man allowed
one last request?''

She wasn't about to be suckered in. ''That de-
pends.''

''On what?'' he asked innocently.

There was nothing innocent about him. There never
had been. ''On what it is.''

He laughed, conceding the round to her. But not
the match. ''You play dirty, Jessi.''

Jessica inclined her head. He'd get no argument
from her. She played to win because the stakes were
too high for her to lose. She'd already used up the
warranty on her heart.

''I know my playing field.''

''Touché.'' And then the teasing smile faded, turning into one that was far softer, far gentler. His eyes

touched her as he asked, "May I kiss you, Jessi? Just once, for old-time's sake?" He saw his answer in her eyes, but waited, anyway.

It was exactly for "old-time's sake" that she didn't want him to. Because it would make too many old feelings surface.

But he'd never asked to kiss her before. Never had to. They'd been drawn together with the force of an attraction that was far too great to resist from the first instant their paths had crossed.

Jessica knew that she should say no. Shout it and slam the door shut. But something within her wanted to see if she was up to the challenge. To see if part of her was really over him the way she'd told herself she was. The way she wanted to believe.

She debated a minute, then acquiesced. "All right, but no hands."

"No hands?" He loved touching her, framing her face with his hands, feeling her skin beneath his fingertips. "I'll be thrown off balance."

But she wouldn't be moved on this. If he touched her face, she'd been a goner.

"That's my deal, take it or leave it." She fully expected him to leave it, to reject the offer and walk off, annoyed that she should put conditions on his request.

He surprised her.

"I'll take it."

The moment his lips touched hers, Jessica knew she should had added "no lips" to her clause.

She wasn't over him. Oh, God, she wasn't over him. Not by a long shot.

If anything, this kiss, so gently petitioned, so tenderly executed, made it even worse. It reminded her how much she missed him. And how undone she became whenever he kissed her.

Logan felt his heart begin to pound so hard it almost made him lose his balance. God, but he'd missed her. Kissing her only made him more acutely aware of the lack of her in his life.

Hardly more than a whisper across his lips, her kiss hit him with the force of a one-two punch to his stomach, threatening to take him all the way to a technical knock-out—a TKO in every sense of the word.

Hunger clawed at him until he felt nothing but a vast yearning in every part of his body. Every part of his soul.

Without fully knowing what he was doing, Logan slipped his hands up around her face, framing it. Drawing her slowly to him as she just as slowly drew out his life force.

Jessica was stumbling, stumbling badly and headed straight for the abyss that was gaping in front of her. How could she have said yes?

How could she have said no?

But no was what she should have said.

No.

In an eleventh-hour attempt to save herself, Jessica jerked her head back, away from his mouth. Away from her impending downfall.

Her body ached. She could have wept with vexed frustration.

"You cheated." The words were hoarse, having fought their way up a throat that was bone dry and aching. Just like the rest of her. "You used your hands."

"Sorry," he murmured, only half-aware of what she was talking about. He hadn't cheated, he *felt* cheated. "I lost my head." It took a minute before his pulse stopped vibrating sufficiently for the beats to actually separate themselves enough to be counted. "I'll do better next time."

She dragged a deep breath into her lungs. It didn't help. She felt no calmer, no more composed. "No next time. Once is enough."

Once is *more* than enough, she added silently. She was surprised she was standing.

His smile enveloped her, drawing her perilously close again. "That's not what you used to say."

The break had to be clean, quick, before she weakened altogether. "Good night, Logan." Jessica firmly closed the door in his face.

Logan stood staring at the barrier for a moment, then slowly smiled to himself just before he turned away. He could still taste her on his lips. She was just as heady as ever.

Maybe even more so because now she was forbidden fruit by her own decree.

He doubted very much if he was going to get any sleep tonight.

With the door closed between them, affording her

some respite, Jessica finally unlocked her knees. She'd done it to keep from literally melting into his arms. The man's mouth should be registered with the local police department as a lethal weapon.

Her back pressed against the door, she literally felt herself pour down to the floor, temporarily drained.

One day down and four more to go, her brain echoed. Four very long days and four even longer nights. The distance from here to there seemed almost insurmountable right now. Jessica touched her mouth with her fingertips. She could feel her lips still tingling. Hell, she could feel her body still tingling.

She doubted very much if she was going to get any sleep tonight.

"Just like old times, eh, Jessi?"

When she shook her head uncomprehendingly on the dance floor, then cupped her ear, Logan raised his voice and repeated the question. Even though it was a Wednesday night, the noise in the nightclub, The In Place, was close to deafening. It was hard to believe that he'd thrived on this, night after night, not that long ago.

"Not quite," she all but shouted back.

She'd hoped they would have called it an evening, after Logan had accompanied her to question another member of the board. It was well after eight when they'd arrived back at his house. But he'd turned around and told her that he was going out for a few hours to unwind. It didn't surprise her. He'd always seemed limitless when it came to energy. Unable to talk him out of it, she'd had no choice but to change and go with him.

The look in his eyes when she'd come down the stairs wearing a very short silver dress almost made it worth it for her.

They'd come here against her wishes and her advice. She couldn't protect him in a crowd, and she didn't like the idea of having him exposed like this. But he had insisted. It was almost as if he was determined to go over all the old ground they'd once covered together, frequenting clubs and restaurants where once they'd come as lovers. It wasn't going to do him any good, she swore.

Right now, it wasn't doing her much good, either.

Just before he'd asked her to dance, she'd caught him looking at her in that old way of his, the way that used to make her think he could read every stray thought in her head. But he couldn't. Not now. She wasn't that transparent anymore.

Oh, wasn't she? The question throbbed in her mind, imitating the beat of the music.

"It could be like old times."

He didn't have to elaborate. She knew what he meant. They'd capped off every evening the same way. In each other's arms.

"You're forgetting why I'm here." She intended to do her job and let it end there. Anything else wasn't possible. And definitely was not wise.

"I'm trying to." And doing a damn fine job of it, he thought to himself.

The song ended. Another took its place instantly,

one piece hardly discernible from the next. Logan took her hand and then began weaving through the throng of moving, pulsing bodies. Places like this didn't really stir him the way they once had. But he thought that reliving this with him might make her remember the way they'd once been. Partying was almost all they'd done when they were together. That and making love. In his mind, he supposed, the two were still linked. No one could fault him if he hoped it was the same with her.

Because he found himself wanting her more and more with each passing hour.

Even as she followed him from the dance floor, Jessica could feel the music throbbing in her body. Or was that her own growing desire, demanding to be freed? She was beginning to feel she couldn't tell the difference. Which was a very bad sign.

Turning to look at Jessica now, Logan allowed his eyes to sweep down the length of her slowly. The light in the nightclub was fairly sparse, but what there was of it was gathering around her, its beams scattering off her dress and making it flash with every movement she made.

Much the way her eyes did.

The dress was held up by two very flimsy-looking ties that made his hands itch and his mind wander into regions that could get him slapped.

He saw her looking at him, bemused. He held her a little closer as he smiled into her eyes. "I'd forgotten just how long your legs were."

It was a lie. Though he'd tried more than once, there was absolutely nothing about her that he'd forgotten. Especially the way holding her had made him feel.

"Long enough to get me where I want to go. Speaking of which," she glanced toward the door. From here she could barely make it out. "Are you ready to leave yet? I think I've had enough."

He nodded. "Maybe you're right. It's getting too hot in here." The warm press of bodies had quickly evaporated any cool air around them less than five minutes into their arrival. The hour they'd remained seemed longer.

Ushering her toward the front, Logan shepherded her out, using his own body to block other people who got in their way. Jessica wasn't happy about the reversal in roles.

"I'm supposed to be the one protecting you," she said into his ear. If they were any farther apart, he wouldn't have been able to hear her.

Logan winked at her. "I'll let you make it up to me later," he promised.

The man never gave up, she thought.

Pushing the heavy door open, Logan held it there as he let her walk out first.

As they stepped outside the club and past the guard at the entrance, a blast of cold air went right through them.

The same, fortunately, couldn't be said for the two shots that were fired.

* * *

The man in the alley felt pain, dull and throbbing, traveling from the man's hip down to his right calf. Both his legs were beginning to feel stiff and his back was aching.

He wasn't used to standing like this. Not unless he was leaning against a crap table. Damn it, where *was* Buchanan?

Maybe he should have hired someone to do this. But no, that would only leave him open to blackmail, and he was in enough trouble already.

How, how had he come to this place in his life? Desperate, hunted.

He didn't want to die.

Perspiration poured along his body, even though the evening was cool. The scent of onions clung to him, a telltale marker of his fear.

No one had seen him hugging the shadows of the alley across from The In Place. The activity was all over there. Here, in the alley, it was desolate.

Except for that one old wino who had come into the alley to relieve himself. The filthy smell had almost made him retch.

But the old man had ambled off, clutching his torn-paper-bag-shrouded cheap anesthetic, oblivious to the man who was barely inches away from him.

His head was aching. Adrenaline pumped through his veins, and his eyes flickered, alert, every time he saw the door to the club open. But every time, he was disappointed. It wasn't Buchanan.

Were they going to stay in the damnable club all night?

Chapter 9

The instant she heard the loud, popping noise, Jessica threw herself against Logan, pushing him to the ground and knocking the air out of him. Rolling on top of him, she shielded him with her body.

The crowd restlessly milling outside The In Place, waiting to gain entrance, reacted to the sudden evasive action. They screamed and squealed, scattering like multicolored leaves in an unexpected blast of wind and diving for any cover they could find.

Tuning them out as best she could, Jessica scanned the area, looking for the shooter. There was no doubt in her mind what the sound belonged to. Still on top of Logan, she twisted and pulled out the Smith & Wesson from her purse. She felt him moving beneath her.

Logan's head ached where it had made contact with

the pavement. A little dazed, he was still very aware
of her. He would have had to be dead not to. Slipping
his arms around her, Logan held her to him.

"Why Jessi, this is so sudden."

She didn't bother to look down at him. Frustration
echoed through her. There were too many people in
the way for her to make anything out.

"Shut up, you idiot. Someone just took a shot at
you."

He thought she was overreacting and causing a
panic around her. How could she discern a gunshot
from the rest of the din? He hadn't heard anything.

"Jessi, there's nothing but noise out here. It was
probably just—"

This wasn't the time to get into a discussion about
acoustics. "I know gunfire when I hear it."

Cautiously, gun still drawn, she looked around one
last time before finally easing off his body. She remained crouching as she scanned. Despite her heightened awareness, or maybe because of it, every inch
of her body that had come in contact with his vibrated
like a sharply plucked harp string.

Scrambling to a sitting position, Logan brushed
himself off. The large bouncer who ordinarily stood
guard at the door made his way over to them, crouching as low to the ground as he could manage. He
reminded Logan of a gorilla, policing his territory.

"What's going on?" The nervousness in his voice
was inconsistent with his size.

Jessica rose to her feet at the same time Logan did,
ignoring his outstretched hand. The cars parked at the

curb were empty. The alley was the only possible place the shots could have come from. Muttering an oath, she sprinted in that direction.

Damn, now what? Logan was quick to follow her. "We're making a movie," he tossed over his shoulder to the bouncer.

A sheepish look washed over the wide face as the man, obviously feeling foolish, stood up again. His hands were fisted at his waist as he shouted after Logan. "Oh, yeah? Then where're the cameras?"

Logan didn't bother creating an answer for him. He was too worried about Jessica. If someone was shooting at them, she should be running from the gunman, not toward him.

"Jessi," he yelled after her, "are you out of your mind?"

The next moment he was forced to come to a skidding halt behind her. She was at the mouth of the alley, her gun raised and poised like so many movie cops he'd seen, making her way in by inches. He could swear she'd even stopped breathing. He knew *he* had.

She didn't spare him so much as a look. She couldn't afford distraction. "Damn it, Logan, stay back," she hissed in a low whisper.

"And let you have all the fun?" he asked against her ear. "Not on your life." He wanted to be there to protect her if anything happened. Logan stared into the darkness, not seeing anyone.

A second later a cat screeched, knocking over some debris and tripping over a stray, metal garbage can lid. The resulting clatter set jarring shock waves through both of them. The animal almost got himself shot for it. Realizing at the last moment that it was a cat, Jessica lowered her weapon.

She let out a long breath. There was no one in the alley. Only a lingering stench she tried to place. Probably just the garbage.

Whoever had fired at them, at Logan, was gone.

It was only then that she glared at him. How could she protect him if he insisted on shadowing her every movement?

"This isn't 'fun,' Logan." Leaving, she put the safety on and shoved the gun into her purse again. "And it would have been your life if the shooter was any kind of a marksman."

Annoyed, not waiting for him to reply, she hurried back across the way to the front of the club.

The long, curling line was reassembling itself slowly as people warily trickled back, their desire to enjoy themselves outweighing their fear. The smell of panic faded, giving way to the scent of excitement.

The bouncer met her half way. "C'mon, where've you got the cameras stashed?"

Jessica shook her head uncomprehendingly. "Cameras stashed?"

"Yeah," the bouncer insisted. He looked at Logan as the latter came up behind her. "For the movie you're making."

Turning, Jessica looked expectantly at Logan. "Movie?"

Broad shoulders moved in a careless shrug beneath

Logan's navy jacket. "Seemed like the thing to say at the time."

Maybe it was at that. It was better to avoid panic, she thought, and since they couldn't afford to call in the police, because of the bomb threat, Jessica let the impression stand.

She pointed vaguely around. "They're out of sight, to add realism."

Looking off in the general direction she'd indicated, the burly man looked properly impressed. She moved past him and began to examine the front of the wood-trimmed building.

Logan joined her. He glanced at the building but saw nothing. "What are you looking for?"

She didn't answer immediately, concentrating hard as her eyes swept along the boards. If the front had been made of stucco, it would have been harder. And then she found the holes.

"These." The single word rang with triumph.

Taking out a Swiss Army knife from her purse, Jessica dug out first one bullet, then another, from the wall just to the right of the entrance. She had to stand on her toes to do it and still had to reach up high.

Finished, she looked at them thoughtfully. They had both been fired far too high to have hit either her or Logan. Which meant only two things. Either the shooter had a perception problem, or he wasn't aiming to hit either one of them.

If it was the latter, why?

Another riddle. But at least neither one of them was

hurt. Dropping both spent slugs into a handkerchief, she looked at Logan.

"More things for the lab," she murmured. She would send the slugs out first thing in the morning. Albert was going to love hearing about this.

Logan pretended to be more taken with the contents of her purse. "What else do you have in there?" He tugged on it. "A high-powered rifle, a pup tent?"

She slipped the handkerchief and its contents into her purse. "Just the essentials." She closed it. "C'mon," she motioned him to follow. People were staring at them. For all she knew, whoever had fired at them had slipped into the crowd to watch them firsthand. The thought made her uneasy. "Let's get out of here."

"My sentiments exactly." Catching up to her in one stride, he took her elbow.

"Hey, just one take?" the bouncer called after them as they left.

The man looked ready to ask for a walk-on. Jessica kept moving. "Just one," she called back. "It was perfect."

Logan had to hurry to keep up with her.

When they found his car in the back lot, Jessica raised a hand against Logan's chest, silently warning him to stay back.

"What's the matter?" Looking around, he didn't see anyone except the disgruntled valet they had by-passed.

Opening the door, she checked out the rear of the

car's interior. "I just want to make sure the back seat is empty."

He amused himself by watching the way her body moved as she conducted her search. No doubt about it, the woman looked good coming and going.

Logan stepped back as she straightened again. "This line of work makes you paranoid, doesn't it?"

She shut the rear door and opened the passenger side. "You were just shot at." Getting in, Jessica tugged the seat belt into place. "I have a right to be paranoid." Her eyes followed him as he rounded the hood. "It wouldn't hurt you to have a healthy dose of it, either."

Logan slid in behind the wheel. "Isn't that a contradiction in terms?"

She wasn't in the mood for word games. "Don't get technical on me."

The brief contact between their bodies, enhanced by the pulsating excitement of imminent danger in the air, had only heightened Logan's awareness of her and of his own desire.

"What *should* I get on you?" He started the car. "Speaking of which, I'm beginning to think maybe I should be grateful to whoever was firing at me. At least it got you to jump on me."

They sped out of the lot. Logan had a habit of wanting to conquer every stretch of road he came in contact with, she thought. "I'll jump all *over* you unless you start taking this seriously."

He slowed down as they melded into light traffic. "I am taking it seriously, Jess. I'm just not letting it paralyze me.'' He glanced at her. The illumination from the streetlights glowed along her face, playing hide-and-seek with the shadows that alternately passed through the car. ''And if he's such a lousy shot, I don't have anything to worry about.''

They were lucky, that's all. ''You have *plenty* to worry about. Those shots were fired at you from across the way. Next time he might be closer.'' The thought gnawed at her. The stakes had just gone up. ''Maybe he's a better shot close-up.'' She fervently hoped not.

Logan put a positive spin on the situation. ''I guess that means you're going to have to stick even closer to me.''

She laughed shortly. ''If I was any closer to you, Logan, you'd be wearing me.''

The grin she saw spreading along his mouth told her she'd walked right into that one.

''Gets my vote.'' Stopping at a light, Logan ran his hand along his neck, rotating his shoulders slightly. It was enough to draw her attention.

Jessica caught her bottom lip between her teeth. ''Did I hurt you?''

He shrugged carelessly. A dull pain whispered along his shoulders. He was going to hurt like hell tomorrow, he guessed.

''You didn't, but the pavement did.''

The light was an inordinately long one. Taking his chin in her hand, Jessica moved his head toward her so she could get a better look at him. Drop-dead gorgeous, as always.

"No cuts or bruises to speak of," she pronounced, dropping her hand.

He shifted in his seat, trying to get comfortable. "None that are visible at any rate."

She'd at least had him to break her fall. He'd only had hard cement. Jessica had no doubt that he was going to hurt. "Soak in a hot tub when you get home."

"Join me?"

The question throbbed with sensuality she found almost impossible to resist. She did her best. "Only if you're coming apart."

Unwilling to give up, he looked at her and played the game a little longer. "Emotionally or physically?"

The man was incorrigible. Jessica pointed at the light. "It's green, Logan. Shut up and drive."

"Yes, ma'am," he intoned obediently.

Closing her eyes, Jessica let out a huge sigh and sank back against the seat. They'd been lucky. This time. But what about next time?

The cold chill that snaked up her spine went deep into her bones, refusing to leave.

She went through the ritual of getting dressed for bed, even though she knew it was futile. She was far too keyed up to fall asleep. Exhausted, Jessica gave it a try, anyway.

Still tossing and turning an hour later, she found she was right. Sleep was miles away from coming. Staring at the ceiling, she wondered what to do with

herself. She hated being inefficient with her time, and
nothing made the night longer than inactivity. She
didn't want to just lie here, thinking and worrying
about Logan.

Maybe—

There was a light tap on her door. Jessica bolted
upright, instantly alert. It was almost one o'clock in
the morning. Not knowing what to expect, she hurried
to the door and opened it.

Logan stood there, looking far more sobered than
she'd ever remembered seeing him—except for that
last evening.

The memory drove thorny spines through her. She
grasped them, knowing she was going to need them
to keep her on the straight and narrow.

Slowly, one tension left her body, only to be replaced by another. "I thought you were going to soak
in a hot tub."

Logan didn't answer immediately. She was wearing a lavender sleeveless nightgown that, though
loose, seemed to slip and slide lovingly along every
slight curve of her body with each breath she took,
each movement she made. He was having trouble
finding his tongue.

"Too restless to soak," he said finally. "May I
come in?"

She didn't think that was wise, but blocking his
way seemed hopelessly Victorian. Making the best of
it, warning herself not to weaken, she stepped back.
"It's your house."

He caught the terse note in her voice and wondered

if they were adversaries again. Too much had happened tonight for him to allow that.

Walking in, Logan was aware just how vulnerable he felt right now. Not because his life had been threatened. He'd raced cars, he understood facing a certain degree of danger. But because he suddenly felt needy. And needing her.

He turned to face her. "I realized that I hadn't thanked you for saving my life."

She shrugged away the words. The strap of her nightgown slid off her shoulder. She tugged it into place, aware that he was watching her.

"I'm just doing what Dane's paying me for, and we've already established that unless you'd suddenly decided to sink a jump shot, there's no way that gunman could have hit you."

"Damn it, Jessi, just let me say thank you." He didn't realize how frayed his temper was until he had snapped the words out.

"All right," she replied almost primly. Jessica folded her hands in front of her. "Say it."

She made him want to laugh. She made him want to shake her. "Thank you."

Jessica covered the doorknob with her hand, her message obvious. She wanted to usher him out. "Anything else?"

Reaching over her head, he pushed the door shut, surprising her. The look in her eyes warned him not to make a mistake. He forged ahead, anyway.

"Yes, there's something else. I've been doing a lot of thinking. Since you came back into my life—"

She stopped him right there, wanting things perfectly clear between them. "I didn't 'come back,' Logan. I'm just visiting. Long enough to keep you safe until your meeting on Saturday. After that, I'm gone." Try as she might, she couldn't make herself sound as impersonal as she wanted to.

Did she mean it? If he stood aside, would she leave once this was over and never look back? Well, they'd find out soon enough, wouldn't they?

"Okay," he said evenly. "Fair enough. I won't stop you." He wouldn't beg. Nothing and no one was worth that.

Her eyes narrowed as she looked up at him. "You couldn't."

No, he thought, he couldn't. Even if he tried to keep her back physically, which he wouldn't, it was her spirit that dictated the situation. And that could never be overpowered.

"But while you're here," he pressed on, "why don't we declare a truce? A *real* truce," he added before she could say anything to contradict him. "We're on the same side in this, but I feel like I'm walking into an armed camp every time I'm around you."

Was he really that thick? Or was it that he just had no memory?

"Sorry, Logan, but that's your own doing. I'm just trying to protect myself."

"Protect yourself?" he repeated incredulously. She was wearing it, he realized. Wearing the scent that he loved. The scent that always made him think of her.

Weaving into his senses, it was clouding his mind. "From what?"

"From you." Jessica could feel herself back on the tightrope again. And in real trouble. "You're like a guerrilla fighter, running in for a sneak attack, then running off again to fight—or make love—another day."

Was that how she saw him, as some heartless womanizer? He'd cared about her while they'd been together. Cared as much as he was able. As much as he'd allowed himself. Maybe even too much. It surprised him that, intuitive as she was, she hadn't sensed that.

"Not a very flattering image."

What did he expect? She tried to shrug carelessly. "You created it."

He moved a little closer to her. A little closer to the heart she'd never managed to fully shield. "Then I can tear it down."

Like the fighter she'd always been, she stood her ground even as she felt it slipping away from her at an incredibly fast rate.

"Not here, not now. Not with me."

He combed his hand through her hair, cupping her cheek. He could feel her trembling. Or was that just his anticipation?

"Why not? I never knew you to be unfair, Jessi."

She meant to jerk her head away. She couldn't quite manage it. "Maybe we weren't together long enough for you to learn that about me."

"Oh, but there now you're wrong. I learned everything I needed to know about you in the first few minutes I knew you.'' The words were soft, sensual, seductive, as they left his lips. ''That you were kind and sweet and had the kind of smile that melted a man's kneecaps at thirty paces.'' His eyes made love to her. ''You also had the best-looking body, bar none, that I had ever seen.''

Lines, all lines. She was trying very hard to remember that. To remember the pain when they broke up. All she could remember was wanting him. ''I was wearing a two-piece suit.''

Maybe she didn't remember all of it. ''It was blue and pasted to your body because of the rain, remember?'' It had been some kind of silk. All he knew was the way it had clung to her. ''I just filled in the blanks, that's all.'' He tilted her head up so that their eyes met. ''And I wasn't wrong.''

She could feel her heart pounding the way it had when she'd run into the alley. More. She'd been in a lot less danger, then.

''But you're wrong now,'' she told him. ''Wrong to be thinking what you are.''

''Am I, Jessi?'' His hands slipped from her face and went around her back. It was a gentle movement, achingly tender. He drew her closer to him still. Until their heartbeats blended. ''Am I?''

She moved her lips, but when the word ''yes'' came out, it wasn't in answer to his question. At least, not the one he'd asked out loud.

Chapter 10

Yes.

If the word lingered on her lips softly, it screamed through her blood the moment Logan embraced her and brought her to him. The moment his mouth came down in sheer wonderment on hers.

Yes!

The exclamation echoed, solitary, unadorned, in surrender, in triumph, as she felt his hands slowly slip along her body, possessing her. Owning her, yet, oddly worshipful, as if he couldn't believe what was happening.

He wasn't the only one.

Logan felt his gut quickening the moment he touched Jessica, the moment he brought her to him. Like someone swimming underwater, he passed his hands over her languidly, unable to move quickly, though his body begged him to.

It was as if he was afraid this was all a dream and that moving too quickly would force him to wake up. The way he had so many other nights before. Dreaming of her. Having her vanish just as he reached out to touch her.

She didn't vanish.

She wasn't a dream; she was real. She was here, in his house, in his arms, and the realization slowly tore away the layers of restraint he'd imposed on himself. Tore them away until they no longer existed.

Over and over again, his mouth slanted over hers. Like a prisoner allowed to walk in the sun again after so many years of darkness, he immersed himself in her. Wanted to drown himself in her.

Jessica bit back a moan. Logan's hands felt as if they'd burned right through the thin material that separated them.

To keep her balance as the world began spinning, she dug her fingers into his shoulders. Her head dropped back when he pressed a single kiss to her throat—then did it again. Over and over he kissed her until she felt disembodied, part of the lovemaking and yet able to hover above it. To watch, anticipate and revel.

Every fiber of her being throbbed, calling to him. Wanting what only he could give. There'd been no one else to take his place after they'd gone their separate ways. No one else to help her forget. Jessica hadn't wanted anyone. She had never wanted anyone before there was Logan.

She wanted now.

He wanted to feast on her. Devour her. An old poem echoed, piecemeal, through his brain. Something about devoting a century to the worship of each part of her. It didn't seem so far-fetched now. But restraint was a slippery substance that was beginning to slide quickly through his fingers.

Logan kissed her eyes, her neck, her shoulders, savoring the taste of her. The essence that was only Jessica.

"I've missed you, Jess," he whispered as he branded her with his mouth. "Missed you more than I thought humanly possible."

The words, ushered in by his warm breath against her skin, burned into her body. Was it her imagination? Or had he actually said them?

In her right mind, she wouldn't have been able to picture Logan saying that he missed anyone. *Feeling* as if he missed anyone.

But she wasn't in her right mind, or any mind at all. She was his, body and soul, and all her flimsy promises to herself notwithstanding, she knew in her heart that she'd come home.

Impatient to have all of her, to see her, Logan tugged at the silky material that clung to her body, underlining every heave of her chest, every breath she took. Very slowly he raised the hem of her nightgown and pulled it up, over her head. Exciting himself beyond words. The nightgown moved like a shimmering lavender wave, withdrawing from her body like the tide withdrawing from the shore.

His fingers suddenly numb as he looked at her, he dropped the nightgown to the floor where it pooled, forgotten.

She was even more beautiful than he remembered. Logan felt his breath struggling in his throat. For a moment he could only look at her.

"If I start making strange noises, it's because I've swallowed my tongue," he confessed.

A smile curved her lips. Taking hold of the sweatshirt he had on, she yanked it from him far more quickly than he'd undressed her. She knew her eagerness was showing, but for now, Jessica didn't care. It was past the time to play games. And he knew by now that she wasn't playing hard to get. Not where he was concerned.

"You've seen me nude before."

He wove his fingers through her hair. "Yes, but you can see the sunset a thousand times and it can still leave you in awe."

The smile on his lips melted her resolve. Her heart was racing as she tried desperately to hang on to at least a little composure. "You always did know what to say."

But he didn't always know what to say, Logan thought. Once, none of the right words had come out. Only the wrong ones.

He placed his finger to her lips. "Shh," he whispered.

Then, to ensure her compliance, he pressed his lips

to hers, kissing away any protest, any further dialogue between them. He didn't want to talk. Didn't want anything to steal the moment away.

He didn't have to dwell on that to know he wouldn't be able to endure it.

When her hands suddenly stilled at his waist, he wondered if she'd grown shy on him. Over and over again in the past two years, he'd imagined her with a legion of lovers, all in an attempt to drive her from his mind. Her slight hesitation made all the doubts, all the unspoken jealousies vanish. And made him glad. He knew he had no right, but he wanted her only for himself. Only true to him.

Placing his hands over hers and coaxing, he guided her fingers to the band of his sweatpants. He felt her smile curving beneath his lips just before Jessica obliged and finished undressing him with a quick sweep of her hands.

Logan shivered as he felt Jessica's fingers tugging away the light gray material from his hips.

Her palms came in contact with his skin. Raising a eyebrow, she drew her head back to look at Logan. "You're not wearing any underwear."

"I was going to bed," he said thickly a moment before he pressed his lips to her throat again.

She tasted of honey and some sweet, tempting fragrance that made his senses swim. He wanted to consume her whole, to move quickly before she disappeared like smoke.

"You still are." Her words came out in a gasp.

She couldn't talk straight, think straight when he was kissing her like this.

The air was racing from her lungs, leaving very little for her to draw on. The press of his mouth along her skin, of his hands moving feverishly over her body, robbed her of her breath, leaving only liquid fire in its place.

She wanted him.

Wanted him to make love to her. With her. Sweet, exquisite love the way only he could.

The way she needed.

She was trembling. It only intensified the feelings that were running rampant through his body. His mouth sealed to hers, Logan lifted Jessica up in his arms and carried her to her bed.

Placing her down gently, he lay down beside her. It felt as if no time had passed, as if all those agonizing nights and empty days that he'd tried to ignore had never been. She was here and he was with her. And if tomorrow still held hoary uncertainties within its hand, he didn't have to think about them. All he wanted to do was think of now.

And Jessica.

Jessica turned her body into his, reveling in the feel of his flesh against hers. Reveling in the promise of what was to be.

No matter what paths they took after tonight, she knew that he'd always be home to her. Two years she'd spent trying to deny it. Two years telling herself to move forward, to get on with her life. But this, she knew, was where her life force emanated from.

His hands combing through her hair, Logan slanted his mouth against hers again. Each time he kissed her, his blood heated a little more, pulsing through his body, urges and demands pouring through in its wake.

They rediscovered each other. Rediscovered all the points where pleasure hid just below the surface, waiting for release.

Waiting for a touch.

A very special touch.

A part of him watched her in awe as she twisted and turned beneath his hand, arching into it as if she were absorbing every last bit of joy, every last bit of pleasure, that could be gotten from what was being created between the two of them. Seeing her like this fed his own joy, his own pleasure. And brought him perilously close to his own precipice.

He knew if he wasn't careful, he'd fall and be lost.

When she reached for him, her hand dipping low, he put his hand over hers, stopping her.

"Not yet," he warned.

Before she could ask why, he pressed her back against the bed, looming over her. Jessica held her breath as she saw the look in his eyes. It burst away from her the next moment, exploding with the ecstasy he'd brought her to.

Logan created magic with the merest flick of his tongue along her body. Magic and fire that coursed along her skin instantly in the wake of the path he forged with the gentle nipping of his mouth and the hot touch of his tongue.

Unable to remain still, Jessica twisted and turned. She grasped the comforter beneath her fisted hands as he primed her for the final ecstasy, bringing her to it so quickly that she lost her bearings.

Jessica gasped his name, then silently pleaded with him using only her eyes.

Logan drew the length of his hot, throbbing body along hers, teasing, foreshadowing. Making her completely crazy as anticipation fed desire.

And then, because he knew he couldn't hold himself back any longer, Logan slipped inside her. A sword sheathing itself in the scabbard that had been fashioned for it alone. A man returning to where he belonged. The excitement of it threatened to make him explode before he was ready.

His final goal was pleasure. Her pleasure. And in gaining it, he had his own.

He groaned as he felt her fingers flutter along his back, searching for a place to anchor herself. Her nails raked along his flesh as they both scrambled up the summit. Eager.

The rhythm was both eternal and scarcely a moment old, the sensations, both familiar and completely brand-new.

Arching her body into his, Jessica frantically began to mimic his movements, desperate for the final climax, the final joining on a higher plain than just the bed they were on.

And when it came, descending like a fiery blanket over both of them, it was almost too sweet to endure. The bed shook beneath them, and Jessica was vaguely aware of uttering a cry. A cry that echoed into his mouth. It seemed fitting.

Spent, fearful of the loss that would come all too soon, she clung to him, telling herself it was all right. That she'd chosen this and that she now had the control she hadn't had before.

Telling herself that it was all right to love him, if only for a little while.

As long as he didn't know.

Logan didn't want to move. Not because he was exhausted beyond belief, which he was, but because if he did, it would be over. The euphoria, the moment, all of that, all that they'd shared, would disappear and he didn't want it to.

He wanted to hold her to him without thinking about anything except how good it felt to have her in his arms again. But when he heard the small, almost imperceptible noise against his shoulder, he knew he had to be crushing her.

Raising himself up to pivot on his elbows, he looked down at Jessica. Her hair was slightly damp against her forehead, the line of her lips slightly blurred. It made him want her all over again.

He shifted a little more. "Sorry."

Sorry.

The word tore through her like a branding iron against resistant, quivering flesh. Instantly she tried to seal herself off from the hurt she knew had to come. He'd conditioned her that way.

"About what?"

Logan could feel Jessica stiffening beneath him.

And felt himself doing the same in a far more plea-surable way. "About crushing you. I didn't realize I was resting my full weight on you." He smiled down into her face. "You make it hard to think."

"Oh."

She looked as if his explanation had taken the wind out of her sails. "What did you think I meant?"

She turned her face from his, looking toward the wall. It was swallowed up by the darkness. "I'm try-ing not to think."

Maybe it was better that way, Logan mused. Not to think, just feel. Then things couldn't be said that had to be unsaid. Or regretted.

Moving off her, Logan turned and tucked her against his shoulder. Because the night had brought a chill with it that was beginning to register, he reached around her and drew the edge of the comforter over both of them.

"That doesn't sound like you. Not thinking," he elaborated when she looked at him blankly.

Jessica could feel herself growing drowsy. How many times had she fallen asleep beside him like this, after the lovemaking had taken away all her strength?

Too few, her mind echoed. Too few.

"I told you," she said sleepily. "I've done a lot of changing in the past two years."

Her yawn slid along his skin, stirring him. He wanted her all over again. From the very beginning. But then, he'd always been insatiable where Jessica was concerned. He'd never seemed to be able to get his fill of her. Which worried him—when he was able to think.

"All for the better," he murmured against her temple, kissing her softly.

Did he mean that? Or was he just saying whatever popped into his head? Eyes widening, she turned to look at Logan.

He couldn't resist her when she looked like that, like a wide-eyed innocent. Hell, he couldn't resist her, period, and he knew it.

And right now he didn't want to try. "Jessi?"

"Hmm?" She was beginning to drift off again. Though it was foolish and she would never have admitted it out loud, she felt safe in his arms. Really safe.

"Are you up to doing it again?" Even as he asked, he began to press small, quick kisses to the outline of her jaw, making it tingle. And doing a pretty good job on the rest of her.

There was a sparkle in her eyes as she turned to look at him. "The question is, are *you* up to it?"

Eyes shimmering with mischief, Logan grinned. "What do you think?"

A laugh bubbled in her throat. Sleep suddenly vanished as if it had never been an issue. "I think I'm going to have to investigate and see for myself."

"That, dear lady, is one of the best suggestions you've had in a very long time."

Shifting until he was over her, Logan wove his fingers through hers. He held her hands over her head as he began to kiss her heated body, one small area at a time. She began to move beneath him again.

"You're going to regret this in the morning," she warned.

"Oh no, not me. I'm a man of no regrets." The words vibrated against her navel.

Desire curled through her belly, taking all of her hostage.

He had no regrets. That meant something to her, but what, she couldn't piece together right now. Not when her world was being encased in a fresh wave of fire all over again and her brain felt as if it had been turned into a curly fry.

Wriggling, desperate to make him feel as disoriented, as hungry as she was, Jessica managed to reverse their positions until she was straddling him. "My turn," she murmured.

"I've always been a firm believer in women's equality," he enthused, his voice dropping as she began to weave a little magic of her own on him. He felt his belly quiver as he felt her breath skim along it.

An eternity later she snaked her way back up and then sealed her mouth to his. They both knew there'd be little-to-no rest before dawn.

They didn't care.

Jessica and Logan had slipped back into heaven on a two-hour pass.

Morning came, not on tiptoes, but with steel-pointed boots, invading, demanding attention. Jessica awoke with a start. Her cell phone was ringing. She began to get up, only to feel Logan's arm tighten around her, holding her in place.

"Let it ring."

"It might be important."

"That's why you should let it ring." He'd been awake for the past twenty minutes, content just to lie there beside her, his arm completely numbed, listening to her breath.

It was a sound he'd missed.

"But—"

He wouldn't let her finish her sentence or her protest. Instead, he did what he'd done last night in the face of possible dissent. He kissed her words away.

Jessica struggled to pull free. Or thought she did. The skirmish lasted less than a minute and took place in the battlefield of her mind. The fight was lost without a single shot being fired. Aroused, she forgot about the telephone as she sank into his kiss.

An hour later the struggle resumed. "Logan, we can't stay here like this all day."

"Why not?"

"Because you have a company to oversee, for one."

"Dane's due back at ten." He angled around her to read his wristwatch on the nightstand. "He's there already if his flight got in on time," he corrected. "He likes taking charge. It makes him nervous when I'm around."

His words nagged at her. She caught her lower lip

between her teeth. "Logan, did you ever think that maybe it might be Dane?"

"Might be Dane, what?"

"Sending those letters."

He stopped kissing her shoulder and looked at her. Was she joking? "He's the one who insisted on bringing you in on this."

"I know, I know, but just think about it. He sends the letters, hoping to get you to reverse your decision, then hires me to cover his trail."

"And shoots at me? Jessica, he's a little strange at times, but he's not homicidal."

"Maybe he didn't shoot *at* you. Maybe he meant those shots to be over your head. Just to scare you enough to make you change your mind about the merger. You would have done it once, in the blink of an eye."

He looked at her thoughtfully. "No, I don't think I would have. But I guess we'll never know." He shifted, inhaling deeply as her fragrance drifted toward him. "You're wrong about Dane, you know. He was in San Diego last night."

"That's what he said."

Logan laughed and shook his head. "What do you intend to do, interrogate him?"

She knew he found the whole idea amusing, but she was still in the beginning stages of the investigation and it frustrated her.

"Check out to see if he was where he claimed to be, for openers. He didn't have to be the one doing the shooting, you know,'' she pointed out. ''He could have hired someone.''

''Trust me, Dane doesn't know those kinds of people. He flinches at a raised voice. You're barking up the wrong tree.'' Logan shifted toward her, lightly cupping her breast. ''Speaking of barking, how's your bite?''

She pushed away his hand, though she felt herself weakening for the umpteenth time. There wasn't nearly as much force behind the movement as there might have been. ''Logan, we have to get up.''

Undaunted, he moved his hand lower, caressing her belly. The slight increased intake of breath was all the sign he needed. ''Why? It's your job to protect me, right?''

He could make it harder to think than any man she'd ever met. ''Right.''

The smile that was on his lips seemed to feed down to his fingertips as he stroked her. ''And you have to admit, I'm really safe here, right?''

She was breaking every single damn rule in her book. ''Right, but—''

''Then you're doing your job.'' The last words echoed along her lips as he kissed her.

She knew she should resist. But the thought couldn't quite seem to take root.

Chapter 11

"Logan, what happened shouldn't have happened."

The last forty-five minutes were a rushed blur that had passed through Jessica's brain without leaving any telltale markers behind. She'd summoned all her self-restraint to keep from opting for an entire day spent in bed. That was fantasy. This was reality, and the sooner she regained her hold on it, the better for her.

He followed her out to the driveway. "Why? Did I do it wrong?"

Without hesitation, Jessica went to her car. The choice she was silently offering him was obvious. Either he went with her, or they went in two separate cars.

There were always vehicles at his disposal—one of

the perks of his position. After a beat, Logan slid into the passenger side of her car.

"No, you didn't do it wrong." Jessica glanced in his direction so quickly his image hardly registered. Yesterday they'd taken his car, and she preferred hers. She was surprised, however, that he hadn't put up a fuss. Maybe some things about him had changed. Once, Logan had to be behind every wheel. Cars had represented control to him. "You did it perfectly, as if you needed to be told—"

"I do." Reflexes almost had him reaching in the wrong direction for his seat belt. He couldn't remember the last time he'd ridden in the passenger seat. "When it comes to you."

Pausing at the black iron gates, she saw Neil peer out of the security booth, then press the controls. The gates drew apart. "But not the others?"

He was trying to pay her a compliment. That of all the women alive, she was the only one who could shake his world, make him reevaluate his priorities. Why was she blocking it?

"The thought isn't supposed to go that way," he protested.

"Why?" The promise of a magnificent afternoon lingered on the blush of a perfect morning. Jessica could feel her mood lifting even as she tried to remain serious. "Where is it supposed to go?"

Been there, done that, Logan thought, although never with Jessica. He'd never had words with her. They'd always seemed to be in sync, in harmony, even from the very beginning. Which was where part of the terror lay. But he understood that now. He hadn't then.

He turned toward her. The seat belt gave very little. "Jessi, let's not ruin it by arguing."

She took the winding course to the main road a little too fast. Realizing what she was doing, Jessica pressed down on the brake, riding it a moment until the speed leveled off.

"That's what I'm trying to tell you, Logan." Better she said it than he. "There is no 'it.' What happened last night has no strings, no significance—"

It amazed him how some words could actually feel as if they were piercing his skin. "I think it had a lot of significance."

No, don't go there, Jessi, came her cautioning thought. *There's nothing there for you. No party favors, no surprises—except for the worst one.*

Stepping on the brake, she turned toward him. This time the look Jessica spared him was long. And penetrating.

"I would have believed that—once."

That hurt him even more. To feel that she had changed that much. "But not now." It wasn't a guess on his part.

"No," Jessica said softly, almost to herself. "Not now."

Because the silence she knew would follow would be too much for her to endure, she reached for the radio and switched it on. A love song was playing.

Can't get a break, can I? she thought impatiently.

Logan turned the radio down. He wanted to be able

to hear her. And didn't want her to pretend that she didn't hear him.

"Did I do that, Jessi? Did I kill that in you?" Guilt twisted a knife in his gut. Whatever she said, Logan knew the truth. That it was his fault. "That innocence, despite the sophisticated life-style existing around you? That idealism I saw shining in your eyes? Did I kill it?"

The denial hovered on the tip of her tongue. She wanted to say no, that he hadn't meant that much to her to have killed anything, but it was a lie, and lies were things she never could abide. Especially not when the lie was only to help her save face.

"Yes, you did." Her voice was cold, detached. "And it's something you're going to have to live with. Now can we table this discussion?"

He doubted that he could anytime soon, at least not within the recesses of his mind. She'd said, in essence, that last night had meant nothing. And how many times had he wished for women who felt exactly that way? That the lovemaking between them was time pleasantly spent, but then it was time to move on.

So here it was, his wish come true. And he didn't want it.

Be careful what you wish for. The old saying mocked him.

Masking his reaction, Logan shrugged absently. "You're the one who brought it up."

Yes, she supposed she had. Jessica kept her face

forward, afraid of what he might see if she turned toward him.

"Only to make sure you didn't think that I was naive enough to hold you to anything because of what happened. It shouldn't have happened because I'm your bodyguard and that's where it ends."

He knew he should just let it lie, but he couldn't. This was Jessica, and he couldn't. "I thought you were my friend, as well."

The short laugh that escaped sounded little more than a huff of air. "Yes, I thought that, too, once."

But friends didn't just stand there, not saying anything, when their friend just had their heart ripped out in front of them, she thought angrily. Friends comforted, shared. Cared.

He blew out a breath, dragging a hand through his hair. Nobody to blame but himself, he thought. "So, here we are."

"Yes, here we are." *Nowhere.* She turned toward him at the light. "Now, what's on your agenda today?"

He tried to read her tone and found that he couldn't. He used to know her so well, now...

"I'd say getting you to change your mind, but that doesn't look very promising. So let's just leave it at going in to the office for now." His eyes strayed to the digital clock on the dashboard. He had less than an hour to spare. But every minute he'd "lost" had been well worth it. "I have a meeting at eleven to try to drum up some support for the vote."

Grateful for the neutral topic, she leaped at it.

"You really are serious about this, aren't you?" Who would have ever thought that he was dedicated to a cause other than his own pleasure? It still amazed her.

Why was she having so much trouble accepting that? he wondered. Other people might have difficulty seeing him in this light, and he understood that, but not Jessi. She should have understood. He was seeing the situation through her eyes. Thinking about the legions of people who made it possible for him to be where he was.

He could still remember the look on Dane's face when he'd told him that he was opposing him on the merger. Total disbelief and shock. In a way, it did make him smile.

"I said so, didn't I?"

She glanced at him to see if he was getting defensive. Big mistake. A wink met her full blast and curled straight into her belly. Jessica turned away and concentrated on the road.

"You've been known to say a lot of things, but I guess I still have trouble picturing you championing any cause that requires more than a small drop of effort on your part."

He had that coming, Logan thought. He'd spent the first three-quarters of his life being the consummate carefree playboy.

Logan spread his arms as much as he could within the confines of the car. "Welcome to the new-and-improved Logan Buchanan."

A smile tugged on her lips. From where she sat, this side of last night, Logan didn't need any improvement, at least, not in some respects. "So who's going to be at your meeting?"

He'd put the calls in himself, doing away with the impersonal touch—and not allowing his quarry a chance to tender a negative response to his secretary. Logan recited their names.

"Why?"

Familiar with all five, she'd already reviewed their financial records and all the other tidbits Albert had managed to pull from various databases, many of which thought themselves secured. Nothing had come to light. And nothing took the place of the personal touch.

"Because I'd like to sit in on it. Observe them. Sometimes body language says things that credit reports don't."

Logan started to demur on principle, then thought better of it. It wouldn't hurt to have her there. Or anywhere for that matter as long as it was close by.

"And you think one of them might be sending me poison-printer letters?" He thought of the people who were attending. The very idea of one of them being a threat made him laugh.

"Very droll." Approaching the building, she headed for the underground parking structure. "I'm trying everything I can think of."

The look Logan gave her was intense enough to make Jessica glance in his direction. "So am I, Jess. So am I."

She walked into his inner office ahead of him. The first thing that caught her attention was the fax machine on the desk that he'd had brought in for her. There were reams of paper spilling out in front of it. Some had found their way to the floor.

Logan whistled. "Looks like the fax machine gave birth overnight." He silently wondered if whoever was threatening him had changed their approach.

Stooping, Jessica picked up the batch closest to her and leafed through them. The lab reports were in. Nothing useful, just as she'd thought. "They're all for me. From Albert."

"That would have been my guess." He unlocked his desk, glancing at the pile of mail on top of it. Were there any new messages? "Must miss you."

With an armload pressed up against her, Jessica rose to her feet. Albert had found more databases to hack into. "They're the reports he's been researching on the members of the board."

Flipping through his own mail, he looked in her direction. "All their innermost secrets. Makes a man feel naked." None. There were no new letters from his friendly neighborhood terrorist-wanna-be. Breathing an inward sigh of relief, Logan dropped the letters back on his desk. "Speaking of naked—" He glanced toward the sofa.

She remembered. Remembered vividly. A hint of color, equal parts pleasure and embarrassment, crept up her neck. Jessica sincerely doubted that there was any familiar flat surface in the nearby vicinity that they hadn't made love on. He'd brought her here to his office under the pretext of showing her where he worked, when he worked—which was whenever the spirit moved him. That afternoon the spirit had moved him in a far different direction.

To this day, the touch of Italian leather against the back of her thighs brought a pleasurable tingle to her flesh.

Pressing her lips together, Jessica sighed. She found it very difficult to stick to her convictions, when Logan was weaving his way under her skin this way at will. "I doubt very much if the board members would like having you conduct the meeting naked."

He laughed. "Amos Talbot might." He knew for a fact that Amos fervently adhered to a very different life-style than he himself embraced.

Deliberately blocking her mounting feelings and the fact that her body still felt the lingering glow of their lovemaking earlier that morning, Jessica hugged the considerable pile of papers to her. "I have to call Albert."

He knew she was retreating. Maybe it was for the best, actually, he decided. Too much was happening again. Just like the last time. Then it had been a matter of too much too soon. He'd been overwhelmed by Jessica, by his feelings for her. Now, having tried to deny how much he'd missed her and finally coming to grips with it, he found he had things to re-sort in his mind before he could straighten everything out.

Maybe a breather was in order for both of them.

Logan nodded as she sat down at her desk. He took his own seat.

"You do that." There were notes to review, figures

to look over before the meeting. He never liked showing up unprepared for any contingency.

Trying to concentrate only on what she had to do, Jessica tapped out the numbers to her office. She winced as she heard a loud noise on the other end. Albert had picked up on the first ring and started talking immediately before she had a chance to say hello.

"No, I don't know where she is, Mr. Deveaux, any more than I knew five minutes ago—"

What was he doing, shouting her father's name into the phone? "Albert?"

"Oh, it's you." Sarcasm and relief divided up ownership of the sentence. "The missing private investigator. Nice of you to check in with those you left behind in the trenches."

Colorful didn't begin to describe Albert, she decided. She tried to arrange the piles he'd faxed into something manageable.

"I see you've been busy. It looked as if the fax machine had exploded when I walked into the office. Anything pertinent I should be looking at?"

"No new discoveries." He dashed her budding hopes with the offhanded comment. "But I thought you might want to read the reports for yourself—if you can tear your eyes away from tall, dark and handsome long enough to actually focus your pupils."

"My eyes are focusing just fine, Albert. And why did you answer the phone like that?" She slid a little closer to the edge of her chair, drawing Logan's attention to her. "Has my father been calling?"

Her question was met with a disgusted laugh.

"Does the sun rise in the east?" Before she could say anything in reply, Albert sighed dramatically. "The man has been calling me every ten minutes since I walked in at half past eight. Said he couldn't reach you at home and wanted to know where you were. After all these years, he picked a really odd time to care," he added, putting her own thoughts into words. "I didn't know if you wanted your whereabouts to be general knowledge, so I didn't tell him. I see where you get your stick-to-itiveness."

She doubted very much if she'd gotten anything from her parents besides her looks and a few connections. Still, this was not like her father. Complete chunks of time would go by when she wouldn't hear a word from him. Why was he calling?

"Did he say what he wanted?"

"Must be something in the air. First your mother, then your father."

She could tell by Albert's tone that there was a pleased smile on his face. He loved knowing things ahead of her. "First my mother, then my father what, Albert?"

"Your father's getting married and if you ask me, he's nervous as hell."

She stared at the telephone, wondering if she'd misheard.

"Married?" she echoed. There had to be some mistake. Nothing so normal occurred in her father's life. "My father doesn't get married. He's never been faithful a day in his life."

She could almost hear Albert's thin shoulders rustling beneath his sweater. "I'm only the messenger."

"Maybe he woke up one morning, looked in the mirror and realized that he'd let too much of life slip by without making a meaningful commitment," said Logan.

Stunned by his words, Jessica turned around and looked at him. She'd forgotten he was in the room. He was standing behind her.

"Is that our walking target in the background?" Albert asked.

She didn't feel like getting into anything with Albert right now. "I'll call you back later, Albert. Oh, is my father at home?"

"No, but here's the number." He rattled off ten unfamiliar digits to her.

Jessica wondered if the number belonged to her stepmother-to-be as she wrote it down in the margin of one of the reports.

"And please call him before he calls me again," Albert informed her huffily.

She intended to call immediately and get to the bottom of this at least. "Goodbye, Albert. Don't forget to call me if you come up with anything."

"I live to serve."

"Of course you do. I pay you enough." She laughed, shaking her head as she hung up.

Logan leaned a hand on the back of her chair, bringing her attention back to him. "Anything wrong?"

That remained to be seen, she thought. Jessica

tapped the telephone number with the tip of her pen. "My father's getting married."

"So I gathered." Logan turned the chair around so that she faced him. "Why are you so surprised? He married your mother."

Why was it every time she turned around, she felt as if he was closing in on her? Maybe because he was, she mused.

"He said he did that because he was too young to know better." She'd heard that on one of those rare occasions when her parents were actually in the same room. Usually they weren't even on the same continent. It had been the Christmas morning when she was eight. A Christmas she'd sooner forget. A Christmas when her father said his marriage to her mother had been a mistake. "He's had more relationships than a centipede has legs since then."

"Maybe he's decided to have something meaningful in his life."

"My father?" She'd sooner believe that her father had learned how to negotiate walking on water without getting his shoes wet.

Logan saw his reflection in her eyes. Was it an omen? Was there a spot for him in her heart after all? "It's been known to happen."

"Not to anyone I know." She swung her chair back around, forcing Logan to lift his hands from the armrests.

Running her fingers across the keypad, she called the number Albert had given her. The receiver was picked up on the first ring. She was surprised to hear her father's voice on the other end. Over the years, on the several occasions that she'd tried to call him, she'd had to face a veritable battalion of secretaries before she could reach him.

"Dad, it's Jessica."

"Jessica." His voice sounded strangely breathless and pleased. Concern nudged aside her attempt to sound indifferent. "I've been hoping you'd call. Where have you been?"

It seemed rather odd to her that after twenty-seven years her father would suddenly begin worrying about her whereabouts. Not when it hadn't mattered all those years that came before. Years when his concern would have meant something.

She caught herself being impatient and curbed it. "I'm working a case, Dad. Albert said something about you getting married."

"I am." She heard the excitement working to break free. This was her father? "Could we meet somewhere for lunch?"

How many times, as a child, had she longed for at least five minutes worth of attention from either of her parents? Why was this coming now, when it was too late to change anything? Too late to take the past back?

"Today? I don't think I can—"

Hearing herself, Jessica stopped. She sounded just like her father when he'd made excuses. He'd used his life-style to deny her the time she needed. She was about to do him one better and use her work as an excuse. But she didn't want to sound like either

one of her parents. And there was nothing sweet about
revenge, not on this level.

She reconsidered her time frame. "I can meet you
at one o'clock at La Andalucia." The restaurant was
in the outdoor mall three miles from Logan's office
building. Getting there should be no problem for her
father if he was anywhere in the area.

Jack Deveaux was accustomed to calling his own
shots. "I was hoping for—"

She cut him short. "One at La Andalucia or I can't
make it."

A beat went by. "One it is. See you then, Jessica."

"Goodbye." She hung up the receiver, staring at
it and not seeing the telephone at all. What was this
all about, she wondered.

"So, we're meeting your father for lunch?"

Logan's voice brought her back to her surround-
ings. She swung her chair around to face him. "Don't
you have a meeting?"

"Shouldn't take two hours." He'd make sure of it.
He doubted if it would take more than half an hour
to sew these people up. Forty-five minutes tops. "It's
been a while since I saw Black Jack."

Black Jack. A nickname she'd once thought referred to the state of her father's heart instead of his
favorite card game. She adjusted the pile of papers
closest to her. Busy work.

"Join the club."

She looked bemused, he thought, sitting on the
edge of her desk. Was she upset about the wedding,

or was something else on her mind? "I always liked him."

That didn't surprise her. Her father had a knack of getting by on his charm, just like Logan. "You would. The two of you are very alike."

Getting up, he momentarily retreated to his desk. The paper he wanted was on top. Folding it, he slipped it into his inside pocket. "I'll take that to be in a good way. So." He adjusted his jacket. "Ready to go to Bartholomew's." He named a popular restaurant where large deals were rumored to be sealed with a fair amount of regularity. He liked choosing his battlefields. It gave him a psychological advantage. "I find conducting meetings in congenial places relaxes people, so that when I'm ready to strike, they're more receptive. Little something I picked up from my grandfather."

She fell into step beside him as they walked out of his office. "You're just full of surprises today, aren't you?"

"Lady, you have no idea." He stopped by his door, giving her a way out, though he was hoping she wouldn't take it. Maybe it was childish, but he wanted her there with him. Watching him. "Sure you don't want to stick around here?"

Jessica feigned surprise at the suggestion. "And miss seeing you in action? Not a chance."

Logan laughed as he took her arm. "All right, you asked for this."

"Logan!"

They turned to find Dane striding toward them in

the hallway. His thin face was flushed. "Going home so soon?"

"No, going to meet with some of the board."

The genial smile melted into concern. "Logan, I wish you wouldn't go through with this."

Logan looked at Jessica instead of his brother. "Dane's had his turn at them," he explained. "It's only fair, Dane. You remember fair, don't you? That's what you always wanted me to be."

But Dane frowned. "I'm not talking about the merger, Logan. There's more at stake here than a few men losing their jobs."

Before her eyes, Logan became completely serious. He'd really decided to champion this cause, she thought. "A thousand is hardly a few. And I'm sure not a single one of them think that it's such a little thing."

Dane remained firm. "When compared to your life, it is."

But Logan wasn't about to be swayed. Still, he appreciated the concern he saw. He clamped a hand on his brother's shoulder. "Nothing's going to happen to me, big brother. I'll see you later tonight, all right?"

Not waiting for a reply, Logan ushered Jessica toward the elevator. Reaching around her, he pressed the Down button.

He glanced at her. "Still think he's in on it?"

Jessica looked over her shoulder. Dane was still standing there, watching him. The frown on his face had only deepened. "I don't know."

"I do," he said firmly. The door opened. Logan

waited for her to step inside before he joined her. "You've gotten far more suspicious than I remember, Jessi. But you've also gotten even sexier, so I guess it's a trade-off."

Jessica didn't know about that. As a matter of fact, there were a lot of things she was unclear about right now, she thought, as the doors closed again.

Chapter 12

Logan could sense her tension even before he slipped his hand around her waist to guide her through the restaurant's heavy mahogany doors. It had ridden with them, a small, almost imperceptible passenger in the car all the way over from his meeting.

Now, like powdered gelatin dropped into water, it was gaining substance and breadth by the moment.

He inclined his head toward her, whispering, "You all right?"

Lost in thought about her father, Jessica jerked her head up. She looked at him. "Yes, why?" Then she scanned the restaurant. There wasn't much she could see. La Andalucia was known for its dark, soothing atmosphere.

Dark and soothing were annoying right now.

There was no need for elaboration. They both knew why he'd asked. He'd never seen her quite like this before.

"Just checking," he murmured. Like Jessica, he scanned the immediate area, looking for Jack Deveaux. He saw him first. "There he is."

Logan indicated a table in the middle of the restaurant. The man wasn't alone. Logan wondered how Jessica would react to her father's companion. The woman looked to be several decades younger than Jack.

Jessica didn't feel up to this. The meeting Logan had called together at eleven had gone well from his point of view, but had given her no further insight into the situation that faced him. None of the people he'd spoken to seemed the kind to even contemplate writing death threats, much less act on them or fire a weapon. As far as she was concerned, she was left still standing at square one.

And where was she here?

The whole ordeal before her left Jessica unsettled. She was about to meet with her father, a man who'd neglected to attend any of her graduation ceremonies since the time she first attended school. A man who thought a flat piece of paper written out for a large sum of money more than adequately took the place of his presence in her life. And then suddenly, out of the blue, he was calling, asking to see her.

Why?

Logan's arm rested around her waist and was far more comforting than she thought possible. Just having Logan with her helped. It wasn't something she found easy to admit, even to herself.

She wasn't moving. "Nervous?" Logan whispered.

She wasn't about to go that far, even though she had a feeling he knew. *Uncomfortable* was a far better, detached word.

Jessica stared at her father. He hadn't seen them yet. He wasn't even looking for them. Instead, he was sitting with his head inclined toward the woman, their hands joined across the table.

If she didn't know better, Jessica would have called the scene loving.

"Uncertain what I'm doing here," she finally replied in answer to Logan's question.

Logan doubted that. From what he'd witnessed these past few days, uncertainty was the last word he would have used in describing Jessica. She was as decisive as they came. She was also, as he recalled, a much-neglected daughter.

"You're here because he asked you to come." His words were soft, gentle. And on the mark. "And because I think he wants your blessing."

She raised her eyes to his. The idea hadn't really occurred to her. If anything, she would have said her father wanted to show off his latest acquisition. Jack Deveaux was a man without a conscience, a man who did whatever he chose whenever he chose. The thought that he actually wanted something as mundane and old-fashioned as "blessings" from her almost made Jessica laugh. Even as the possibility warmed her.

"My father?"

"Your father. Stranger things have been known to happen."

Slipping his arm from her waist, he took her hand and wove his fingers with hers. The squeeze was meant to fortify her. And to let her know he was there for her.

"It won't be so bad," he promised, just as the hostess approached them. "We see our party," he told the woman, indicating Jack's table. "The table right over there."

Nodding, the hostess picked up two menus from the reservation table. She cradled them against her lean body as she led the way to the center of the crowded restaurant.

Her father always did like center stage, Jessica thought as she saw him stand up. When they approached the table, his aristocratic face seemed flushed with pleasure and anticipation.

"Jessica, I wasn't altogether sure that you'd come." The tiny chip of uncertainty in his voice validated his statement. "And Logan." Taking Logan's hand, Jack pumped it like a suitor, eager to make a good impression. "Nice to see you." Surprise belatedly entered his eyes as he looked from his daughter to Logan. "I didn't realize you two were together again."

That made it a double surprise. She had no idea that her father had ever known about them to begin with, though they'd made no secret of being together. It just wasn't the kind of thing her father would have taken note of. Only her mother with her ravenous appetite for "the right" alliances had jumped on the idea of their "union." Paulette Deveaux must have somehow let her ex-husband know about them, though Jessica doubted her parents communicated very much these days. They'd hardly done that while they were married.

Jessica began to set her father's misimpression straight, but he never gave her a chance. Instead, he smiled broadly and indicated with an even broader sweep of his hand the woman sitting at the table.

"Jessica, Logan, I'd like you to meet Rachel St. Clair." He was actually beaming when he looked at her. "The lady who's about to do me the supreme honor of marrying me."

He sounded more like her younger brother than her father, Jessica thought as she took Rachel's extended hand. It didn't surprise Jessica that Rachel looked only about five years older than she was. Her father liked them young. And he usually liked them far less intelligent-looking than the woman who shook her hand.

She managed to murmur appropriate congratulations with the proper enthusiasm before she sat down. Rachel looked truly grateful.

Albert was right, Jessica thought. There *was* something in the air.

"Do you *have* to go to this party?"

Logan stopped the futile struggle with his tie and turned around to see Jessica standing in the doorway to his room. Shimmering in his doorway he supposed would be a better description. She was wearing a floor-length gown with the most provocative slit he'd ever seen. It came up high enough on one thigh to flirt outrageously with her hips.

The way he wanted to do.

How the hell was he going to keep his mind on the fund-raiser tonight, when his body was going to be begging him all evening to find a secluded place and make love with her? It had been almost two days since they'd made love.

He realized he was staring at her and found his tongue. "It's not a party, it's a fund-raiser, and yes, I do."

Though it took effort, he turned back to the wardrobe mirror and resumed wrestling with his tie.

Even half-dressed, nobody looked better in a tuxedo than he did, Jessica thought, crossing over to him. Standing beside the mirror, she watched his struggle, finding it sweetly endearing for reasons she didn't bother putting into words, even in the recesses of her mind.

Nothing was safe from Logan, least of all her.

"Party, fund-raiser." She waved her hand. "It's all an excuse for people to mingle, cut each other down behind wide smiles and drink too much."

He slanted her a look. Those were offenses he'd never known her to be guilty of. He'd never heard her say an unkind word about anyone or have more than two glasses of wine. But she was in the minority.

"I won't have more than one drink, and I promise

not to cut anyone down—unless he puts his hands on you.'' Finished, he pulled the ends of the tie. Too long and thin, it drooped. He sighed, exasperated. ''Feel better?''

No, she didn't. It had been a very strange day, following on the heels of a very unsettling night. After a surprisingly enjoyable lunch with her father and his fiancée and then tying up some details at the office, she and Logan had gone to his home. She'd been completely prepared to logically rebuff any advances on his part with a list of reasons as to why.

There had been no reason to rebuff. He hadn't come to her last night. She'd lain awake, waiting, but the knock never came.

It was what she wanted, what she *claimed* she wanted, and yet, it had left her worse off than the night of lovemaking that had come before. Tense, agitated, she was having trouble maintaining her cool. She was at a loss as to just what to think about anything right now.

Jessica forced herself to focus on the real reason she was in his life and he in hers.

Pushing his hands gently aside as he began yet another fruitless attempt at the tie, she did the honors herself. ''I'd feel better if you weren't going at all. You can't continue being a moving target, Logan.''

''Maybe we'll flush him out tonight.''

Jessica bit back the protest that she didn't want to flush anyone out, tonight or any other night. She just wanted him to remain safe. And breathing, even if it wasn't with her.

Finished, she stepped back and pretended to admire her handiwork.

"Besides—" he turned to look at her "—I don't do hiding very well, Jessi. And don't forget, I have you to protect me."

How could she forget? It was on her mind constantly. His welfare, his *life,* was in her hands. She frowned impatiently. "I'd do a better job of protecting you if you listened to me."

The shrug was deliberately careless to hide just how much he did care. "Can't have everything, Jessi."

The words struck her as ironic. "You used to think you could have it all."

Their eyes met for a long, silent moment. "I grew up and realized I couldn't." He glanced into the mirror. The tie was perfect. "Nice job," he commented. "For some reason I couldn't seem to get it straight tonight." His smile was sensual, teasing as he aimed it at her. "Must be all those butterflies over having you so close that were throwing me off."

As if she'd ever believe that. "You were born flirting and don't even have so much as a nodding acquaintance with a butterfly."

Ordinarily her comment would have amused him. But this time, because he'd spent the night longing for her, it jarred rather than amused. Doing "the right thing" could be damn hard sometimes. But he wanted to be absolutely fair to her.

Logan crooked his finger beneath her chin. Raising it, he brushed his lips against hers.

"Don't bet the farm on that one, Jess." Out of the corner of his eye, he saw a bewildered look enter her eyes as he reached for his jacket. He shrugged into it. "By the way, I invited your father and your future stepmother to the party. The organization needs every donation it can get," he explained, anticipating her protest. Then, when it didn't come, he looked at her. "Are you all right with that?"

"Yes." The reply was automatic, but then she paused to actually give it some thought. The answer surprised her. "Yes, I really am. I'm glad he's happy." She'd never wished either of her parents ill. All she'd ever wanted was to have a little of them in her life, but that time had passed. "I just don't know which surprises me more, that he's settling down, or that he actually wanted to introduce me to her."

"He wants your approval."

She still had trouble buying into the idea. "Yeah, right."

Logan picked up his wallet from the bureau and slipped it into his pocket. "No, seriously, I really think he does. There was no other reason for him to be that nervous when we got together."

Jessica thought of the lunch. She was accustomed to a fine, polished edge to her father. It had been missing yesterday. The realization coaxed a smile from her. "He was nervous, wasn't he?"

That had been obvious to Logan from the moment he'd seen her father. "Like a man who had put all his money on a risky stock and was watching the market activity for all he was worth.'' He looked at her. ''Maybe you should give him another chance.''

His attempt to bring her together with her father made Jessica look at Logan in a completely new light. She had no idea he cared about things like that.

Tugging on a silver shawl that seemed constructed entirely out of silver cobwebs, Jessica turned to leave. She realized that she had fallen under very close scrutiny and admittedly enjoyed it before she raised a quizzical eyebrow in his direction. There was something on his mind.

''If you don't mind my asking, where are you planning on hiding your weapon? The one with the trigger,'' Logan added with a wide grin. All of her looked like a lethal weapon, he thought. An extremely sexy, overwhelming lethal weapon.

''In my purse.'' She held the small clutch purse up. It hardly looked big enough to accommodate the pistol, but she had bought it with exactly that in mind. And then, prompted by the look on his face, she added, ''Don't tempt me to use it.''

He swept his keys up into his hand. ''Those weren't the kind of fireworks I had in mind.''

No, but they were the ones she was worried about.

''It's not too late to change your mind about this,'' she said.

And as much as she found herself enjoying the nostalgic trip he kept taking her on into the world she used to frequent, she really wished he would change his mind and remain home. It was easier guarding him on a one-to-one basis than trying to have eyes in the back of her head.

"Yes, it is," he contradicted. "My name's on the invitations."

It hadn't occurred to her that was why he was so insistent about attending. She stared at him. "*You're* hosting the fund-raiser?"

Amused at her reaction, Logan presented his arm to her. "None other."

The Logan she knew had always been generous with his money, but his time was another matter. That belonged to him exclusively and he shared it with race tracks and people who had the same interests he did. Charities had never numbered among them.

"Since when?" she wanted to know.

He didn't feel like going into it, or his motives. He'd never liked explaining himself, even when he came off well.

Logan glanced at his watch. "One half hour from now. Shall we?"

Knowing it would do no good to press, Jessica inclined her head and slipped her arm through his.

The packed ballroom made Jessica uneasy. Time and again she'd found herself in scenes just like this one before she'd discovered a purpose for herself. But it had never been while she was responsible for someone's safety.

She recognized a number of people. It didn't help quell the edgy adrenaline she felt pumping through her veins. There were others, many others, she didn't know.

She would be glad when the night was finally over. This having to be constantly on her toes was wearing.

Though women swarmed around Logan like the proverbial bees to honey, he managed to remain within easy range throughout the evening. And periodically, whenever he found himself free, he would drop back to be with her, easily cutting into any conversation she might be having with someone as if he'd been there the entire time. Being charming was not an effort for him, it was a way of life and it suited him like a second skin.

Jessica had to admit that she was surprised at how cooperative he was being. He didn't even dance with anyone else, except for Beatrice Champion and she was near eighty. To all the other women, he'd begged off because of "duties."

That in itself was an overwhelming surprise. Even at the height of their affair, she'd had to share him with others at parties.

Watching him, she thoughtfully ran her fingertips along the brim of her empty wineglass, the one glass she'd allowed herself all evening.

The new-and-improved Logan Buchanan, she thought, remembering the way he'd referred to himself. Maybe he was, at that, at least in some respects.

Logan worked the room like a pro, extracting promises of huge donations to the charity of the evening: The Abused Children Fund. Her father's promissory note was one of the largest of the evening, matched only by the one Logan had put in himself as "seed" money.

She had to admit she was more than a little impressed.

She wasn't there to be impressed, she reminded herself. She was there to watch over him. Nothing more. Jessica set down the glass on a nearby table.

So far it all looked harmless. Everyone was having a good time, some more than others, judging by the wine consumption. There didn't seem to be any threats coming from any quarter.

She wondered if this was destined to be one of those mysteries that would remain unsolved or if someone would tip their hand soon. The vote wasn't that far away and at least from what she had noted these past few days, Logan was networking successfully and making headway in his proposal.

The song the orchestra began playing penetrated. Longing flooded her as she remembered. "Forever, My Love." It was the first song they had ever danced to. He'd softly sung along with it.

She tried unsuccessfully to block the sentimental feelings that were seeping through her.

Logan came up behind her. "Care to dance? They're playing our song."

She turned around, wondering if he remembered or if he was just being flippant. One look in his eyes told her he remembered.

"You can case the joint while you're dancing," he added, taking her hands in his. "Is that the right terminology?"

Moving on pure instinct, she rested her head against his shoulder, letting the music take her away. The music and Logan. "Only if you're a character in a Sam Spade mystery.'' She smiled. ''Are you trying to make me feel at home?''

He felt her smile against his chest. Felt her smile seep into his body. Yearning swept over him quickly. How much longer did he have to remain here, he wondered. How much longer before he could hold her again. Before he could have her again?

''Me, Jessi?'' Logan murmured against the top of her head. ''I'm just the guy who's trying to make you feel, period.''

Jessica lifted her head to look at him. ''Logan,'' she chided softly with far less conviction than she knew was warranted. ''Don't start.''

''Too late for that, Jessi.'' He looked into her eyes, searching for a sign that she agreed. ''We've already started.''

The thing of it was, she knew he was right.

She tried not to be obvious as she shifted her shoulders slightly. Major kinks had settled in, setting up housekeeping. She could feel fingers of tension all the way up and down the base of her neck.

It felt as if they'd been at the party forever. Not only had they been the first to arrive, but apparently they were going to be the last to leave, she noted. Logan was insisting on personally saying good-night to each couple who had attended.

Though she felt taxed, she realized she was also proud of him. An odd feeling to have about a man she kept trying to convince herself didn't matter anymore.

Her feet were beginning to ache, as well. Now there

was a first. She could usually spend hours in high heels. She *had* spent hours in her high heels, she realized with an amused smile.

"Are you sure you're not planning on running for public office?" she whispered against his ear after he'd bidden yet another couple good-night. She watched the man weave beside his wife, who was half his size. Jessica stifled a yawn. She'd been alert and on her toes for a nonstop six hours and it had taken its toll. All she wanted was to have her head hit a pillow. Any pillow.

"You'll be the first to know," Logan promised. "Make sure you're the one behind the wheel, Alison," he called after the woman. In response, the woman held up her car keys, jingling them.

Satisfied, Logan slipped his hand on Jessica's shoulder, turning her so that she faced the entrance. "That about does it," he announced, relieved to finally have the evening over. Good cause or not, he was tired. "We're free to go home."

"That has a very good sound to it," she answered before she realized her mistake. He'd said "home" and she had absently agreed with the description. But it wasn't home, not to her. Only to him. She was quick to change the subject. "I must say I never thought of you as chairing a fund-raiser."

He shrugged it off the way he did any compliment. He wasn't in it for the recognition. Only the final result. "It's a good cause," was all he said. His commitment to it was left unspoken. She looked tired, he thought. Maybe tonight he'd content himself just to watch her sleep. If he could convince her to share a bed with him. "Ready to go?"

She exhaled. It spoke volumes. "More than ready."

Logan laughed as he walked with her to the entrance. "I guess racing you to the car is out of the question."

"Race?" she hooted.

She was lucky she wasn't falling flat on her face. How did he do it? She knew by a comment he'd made that he'd gotten as little sleep as she had last night, yet he looked ready to go another ten hours.

"Logan, I'm so tired I can hardly stand up."

"Well then, there's a quick remedy for that." He scooped her up in his arms, pushing the door open with his shoulder.

Jessica laughed in surprised protest, her arms automatically going around his neck. "No, Logan, I didn't mean—put me down."

He never got the chance to answer her. The crack of a discharging gun ripped the night apart as the bullet that was fired ripped his flesh. A second one went whistling by, barely missing Jessica.

Stunned, Logan felt his arm suddenly become slack as the sensation exploding in his shoulder registered. Blood colored his jacket.

Jessica found herself tumbling to the ground. Swallowing a gasp, she grabbed for Logan's arm and pulled him down with her.

Chapter 13

"Stay down."

Jessica shouted the order at Logan as she pulled out her pistol. She glanced quickly over her shoulder to see if he was listening. The discolored jacket sleeve, darkened with blood, leaped out at her. She felt her heart immediately constrict, then beginning pounding. Hard.

"Omigod, you're hurt."

The pain hadn't found him yet. There was only surprise and an odd numbness following in the wake of the red-hot sensation that had peeled him apart. What he did feel was rage. Complete, unbridled rage.

It wasn't rage because someone could actually be shooting at him. He could handle that. What he couldn't handle was that because of some unbalanced idiot with a gun and a half-baked grudge, *Jessica's* life was being threatened. If anything happened to her because of him, Logan knew he'd be confined to a living hell for the rest of his existence on earth.

"It's nothing."

The dismissal was bitten off. Before Jessica could think to stop him, he snatched the gun from her hand and snapped up to his feet. Logan's eyes challenged the dark, searching, but there was no one there.

No one he could see. "Come out, damn you, come out and face me."

The screech of tires peeling off in the distance was the only sound he heard in reply.

Jessica was so angry, so terrified for him, she had to bite back a host of scathing adjectives about the condition of his brain. On her feet, she yanked him hard, throwing him off balance. It was the only way she managed to pull him to the side of the building.

"What the—?"

Seething, she reclaimed her gun. "Are you out of your damn mind?" she demanded hotly. "Are you actively trying to get yourself killed? This maniac is *shooting* at you."

"Don't you think I know that?" he shouted back.

She scanned the area again, assuring herself that Logan's would-be assailant had gotten away again. Disgusted, more with herself for failing him than with Logan, Jessica stopped him before he could turn from her. "Here, let me see that."

Logan tried to shrug her away, but the motion was not without its price. Pain shot through him. He tried not to wince.

She'd never been shot herself, but she could well imagine what it had to feel like. Vividly.

"Don't play Apache with me," Jessica upbraided him. "It's a gunshot wound—it hurts. You're allowed to grimace and curse."

As quickly, as gently as she was able, she examined the wound. Her heart wrenched at the sight of the blood oozing from it. "Looks like it grazed your skin." Putting her hand in his pocket, she fished out his handkerchief and pressed it to his wound. "Hold this in place. It'll have to do until they put a bandage on it in the hospital. I don't think it's going to need stitches."

She saw the look in his eyes and knew exactly what he was thinking. "We're going to the hospital," she insisted. "I'm not going to argue with you about this."

"I'm not going to argue with you, Jessi." His tone was so calm, so quiet, she knew he was up to something. She didn't have long to wait to find out what. "How many lives could you stand having on your conscience, Jessi? I don't think I could handle any."

She saw someone look out the back door of the banquet hall, stare in their direction and then disappear inside the building again. So much for any useful witnesses. "What are you talking about, Logan?"

He pushed harder against the wound, hoping he wouldn't pass out. He was feeling oddly light-headed right now.

"He said that if we went to the police, he'd retaliate by putting a bomb in one of the buildings.

There's no way we can know where. If we go to the emergency room, you know they're bound by law to report any gunshot wounds they treat to the police." He let out a long, slow breath, trying to hold on to his focus. "I don't think we're dealing with anyone who's bluffing anymore."

Jessica frowned. Neither did she. And as much as she wanted to deny it, Logan was making sense. The emergency room was out.

"All right, since it is a clean wound, maybe I can take care of you." Placing herself beneath his good arm, she drew it over her shoulder and slipped her arm around Logan's back to help support him. "But the first sign of infection, bomb or no bomb, you're going in. Do I make myself clear?"

"Yes, ma'am."

She muttered a few choice words about his meek acquiescence as they made their way to his car in the lot. The fact that he was leaning some of his weight on her indicated to Jessica that he wasn't feeling nearly as hale and hardy as he was trying to make her believe.

Stopping by his car, she partially leaned him against the hood and put out her hand. "Give me your keys."

With effort, he fished them out of his pants pocket, using his left hand. He held them just above her palm. "I can drive, you know."

"Yes, I've seen you." She took the keys from him before Logan could change his mind and give her a real argument. "Many times. Now shut up and save your strength."

She helped him into the passenger seat, wincing whenever he did. Hurrying, she got in on her side.

His head spun a little as she peeled out of the lot. There's a first, he thought, trying not to pass out. Usually, speed made him feel better, exhilarated.

"Save my strength," he repeated, desperately trying to keep things light. "Why? Are you going to make wild, passionate love to me?"

No, but not because she didn't want to, she thought. "The only thing wild and passionate tonight is the way I feel about finding whoever it is who's stalking you."

Stalking. It was an ugly word with a grim reality attached to it. Logan didn't like feeling confined. "The vote's in two days. He doesn't have much time."

"I have a feeling he already knows that."

They didn't have much time, either, she thought. Not together. The same two days applied to her. Once they were gone, so would she. Gone from his life. And he from hers.

She bit her lip as she saw him wince when she took a turn. "Hurt very much?"

"Enough."

If he allowed that small remark to pass, she knew it had to hurt a great deal. "Are you sure you don't want to go—"

"I'm sure," he cut in.

Jessica pressed down on the accelerator. "Hang on, I'll get you home."

Logan mustered a grin as they made their way up the steps to the front of his house. Jessica had made the twenty-five-minute trip in less than half the time, squeaking through yellow lights just before they turned red. A woman after his own heart.

In more ways than one, he thought. Or at least she had been, before he'd screwed things up.

Struggling to keep her balance with him as she took the steps, Jessica raised an eyebrow at his expression. "What?"

"I should take you on in a race sometime." He leaned against the wall as she unlocked the door. "You drove like a pro."

"I picked it up watching you." And in remembering, she'd succeeded in bringing back a torrent of vivid memories. She had a habit of absorbing everything she came in contact with. Him more than anything. And that was her problem.

Logan waited until she opened the door, then followed her inside. "What else did you pick up, watching me?"

"Well, I could have picked up stupidity tonight if I'd wanted to." She pushed the door shut behind her, making sure she was quiet about it. She had a feeling Logan didn't want anyone else up and fussing about him. Despite his condition, or maybe because of it, she felt she'd held back her temper long enough. "What made you jump up like that? Weren't you enough of a target on the ground? Did you have to try to make it easy for him?''

"I wasn't trying to make it easy for him.'' He struggled to curb his own temper. He knew she wasn't shouting at him, she was shouting at her own fear. "I was angry. If that bullet had just been a little to the right, he would have gotten you.''

Her anger vanished. Her? Logan was concerned about something happening to her? A sweetness drizzled through Jessica. But that didn't change that what he'd done was foolhardy.

"He wasn't after me,'' she pointed out. "He was after you.''

That being the case, it was lucky for him that the man was off his mark. He thought of the first attempt outside the club. "I guess he really is a lousy shot.''

She touched the stain on his jacket, not wanting her mind to go any further with the thought than it already had.

"Thank God for that.'' She looked around the foyer. Neither the housekeeper nor the cook had appeared. "Looks like Julia and Maxine are asleep.''

He nodded his agreement. The dizziness had passed. He was beginning to feel like himself again. A shot-up self, but better nonetheless.

"Good thing.'' He glanced at the wound. His handkerchief was badly stained. "Wouldn't want to scare them.''

If he'd been whole, she would have smacked him. "But me you don't mind scaring out of my mind, right?''

He hadn't meant it that way. "You're getting paid for it, remember? Speaking of which, you're fired."

Taking his good arm again, she threaded it over her shoulders, supporting him as she led him upstairs to his bedroom. With infinite patience, she pointed out—again—why he couldn't fire her.

"We've been all through this, Logan. You didn't hire me, consequently, you can't fire me. Only Dane can." She remembered looking for his brother during the fund-raiser. He hadn't been around. "By the way, where was he this evening?"

He let her lead him to his bathroom. Only slightly smaller than the bedroom, the room was done completely in black onyx. Easing himself down onto the rim of the enormous tub, he saw her reflection in the mirror.

"Don't get that look in your eye again, Jess. He didn't want to be competing with me at the party, that's all. Dane was out seeing if he could drum up some support for his side." He looked up into Jessica's eyes and began to get up. "Dane wouldn't do this."

"Sit," she ordered.

Opening the medicine cabinet, she rummaged around until she found what she was looking for. Disinfectant, tape and a roll of bandages. With deft movements, she took them all out, arranging them on the sink.

"No," she agreed, "he wouldn't. Warning shots are one thing. These shots weren't meant to warn."

She wondered where the second bullet had gone to.

It had whizzed right by her. Tomorrow, before people began arriving in the area and life became busy, she was going to go down there again and have a good look around. Maybe she'd find that second bullet she heard.

Very slowly she peeled off his shirt. He caught his breath as she drew it from his shoulder. Empathy had her stomach waffling in response. She tossed the material aside. The shirt was ruined, just like the tuxedo jacket.

"I'm sorry if this hurts."

Inwardly, he braced himself as he saw her reach for the disinfectant. "Do your worst."

She poured the liquid liberally over the cotton, before applying it to his wound.

"My worst would be to bind and gag you until the vote is taken," she informed him. Looking at the wound, she bit back a sound. "You're going to have a scar on that rugged shoulder of yours," she warned. On him, she had to admit a scar had its appeal.

He watched her as she dabbed the disinfectant on his shoulder. "It'll just add to my mystique."

She reached for a second swab. "As if you needed to have something added."

Logan caught her hand between his. "Tell me more."

"And risk having your head swell?" Jessica drew her hand away. "Think again."

"I am." Taking her hand again, he raised it to his lips and kissed it. The look in her eyes told him she was as affected as he was. "I'll be all right, Jessi. I have you to take care of me."

Jessica frowned as guilt returned, big-time. She picked up the rolled bandage and began binding up his wound. "Big help I was. I was supposed to guard you, not let you carry me around."

He turned his head, watching her work. She moved quickly, competently. He wondered if she'd done this before. And for whom.

"Don't worry about it. I'm good as new. I have wonderful self-healing powers."

She raised her head. "Do you?" She looked at him, remembering the words he said to her when he broke off their relationship. She supposed she never really got over them. A wound that refused to mend. "Some of us aren't blessed that way," she said.

Too late he realized what he'd said. And how it must have sounded. "Jessi."

There was a catch in her voice and it took her a minute to make it vanish. She cleared her throat, then tried to look impersonal. "What?"

He wanted to say he was sorry, sorry for ever hurting her. Sorry for having driven her away with a lie. Sorry for so many things and for all the time that was forever lost. Very, very sorry.

But the words still refused to materialize. The apology wouldn't come. Whether it was because it unmanned him, or made him feel vulnerable, Logan didn't know. All he knew was that he started out wanting to say he was sorry and ended up saying, "Thanks for taking care of me," instead.

For a moment, just a moment, she'd thought he was
going to say something else. That showed *her*. She
shrugged, putting the tape, bandage and disinfectant
back into the medicine cabinet.

"All part of the job."

Rising, he closed the medicine cabinet door
abruptly. They'd waltzed around without music too
much tonight. "And if it wasn't? If you weren't being
paid to hover over me as you pointed out, would you
still have done what you did? Or—"

Her eyes met his. He knew the answer to that. Why
did he have to ask?

"I've always been a pushover for dumb animals.
Especially hurt ones." She sighed. She was tired and
her nerves were on the verge of disintegrating. "Now
go to bed."

He glanced toward the king-size bed in the bedroom behind her. It had felt far too empty last night,
despite all his noble intentions. He didn't feel very
noble tonight. Just needy.

"Come with me?"

She did her best to resist. Did even more to appear
as if resisting wasn't even necessary. She doubted that
she was convincing.

"You're not exactly in any shape to make love,
Logan." She walked past him into his bedroom with
every intention of leaving. "You need rest."

"I need you."

Good intentions crashed and burned as she turned
around to look at him. With those three little words,
he'd caught up her soul and held it in his hand.

"Oh, God, Logan, what do you expect me to say to that?"

"Nothing." He cupped her cheek so softly, she felt as if his fingertips were kissing her skin. "Just stay perfectly still and let me do all the work."

A smile bloomed on her lips. "Work is it now?"

"Of the nicest kind." His lips found hers and any thought of further protest died instantly.

The ecstasy overtook her immediately, mocking her for ever having thought she could break its hold over her. She knew she shouldn't be allowing this to happen, not again. Once was already too much. But emotions born in the wake of her fears that he'd been seriously hurt now left her completely unarmed. She needed and wanted him so much that she couldn't help herself.

Or stop herself.

Needs and desires poured through, escaping like so much water from a dam that had suddenly been opened. Flooding her body. Submerging her mind and any protests that still lingered there.

His lips worked along the outline of her jaw, her chin, her throat. Sparks ignited throughout her body. It took everything she had not to clutch at his arms, not to dig her fingertips into his flesh.

She was his. There was no question about it. She knew it.

No matter what came later. What happened in their lives after this Saturday, after the vote was taken and he didn't need her anymore, she would always be his.

"Undress for me, Jessi." The words drifted seductively along her skin. The entreaty called to her, a legendary siren song of old.

Like a woman in a trance she fixed her eyes on his. With slow, languid movements, she began to disrobe. Hands on her hips, she drew the material down. The silver dress snaked down her body like a second skin being shed.

One silver, the other gold, Logan thought, unable to tear his eyes away from her. Beneath the gown, Jessica was nude, just as he'd guessed. He felt his breath catch in his throat, hardly having ventured beyond his lungs.

It took everything he had within him not to reach out for her. Not to take her into his arms and crush her to his body. He didn't think it was possible to want someone so much. But he did. More and more with each passing moment.

His gaze was so intense, she could feel its heat along her skin. The dress pooled to the floor, catching the light. "What?"

"Every time I see you, you're just that much more beautiful."

Jessica grinned. "In that case, by the time I reach a hundred I should be unbearably gorgeous."

She was there already. He felt the palms of his hands grow itchy.

"Way before that, Jessi. Way before that. C'mere," he whispered, extended his hand to her.

She came willingly, slipping into his arms. He pressed a kiss softly to her temple. The tender act spoke volumes. Far more than any passionate kiss. She felt her heart twisting within her breast.

I love you, Logan, she whispered silently in her mind.

His fingers glided gently along the sensitive skin of her breast as he cupped it. Ever so lightly, he rubbed his thumb over the hardening nipple.

Jessica moaned, absorbing the sensation. When they'd made love the day before, it had been all passion, all fire. This time there was such tenderness, such gentleness, it completely undid her.

Logan had always been a good lover, an instinctive lover who anticipated her every move, her every need. But he went far beyond that this time. With every stroke, every motion, every kiss and caress, she felt that there was something between them that had never been there before. Something equally powerful and sweet.

Wishful thinking, she mused. Or, at best, it was a feeling born of the emotionally charged situation they'd found themselves in. He'd been shot at and could have been killed. That obviously made life that much more precious to him. And his lovemaking that much more rarefied.

She could accept that. Respect that.

Very slowly Jessica unbuckled his belt, her own lips questing over his face, over his neck. She traced the outline of his ear with her tongue.

His sharp intake of breath egged her on, making her very blood heat. She wanted him. Wanted him in the worst way. The best way.

And he wanted her.

If nothing else, she had that, Jessica thought. And for now, that was enough.

His own clothing shed, Logan caught her hand in his and drew her to the bed.

He wanted to make love with her all night.

He wanted her now. This minute, before his own needs made him explode.

Desire plundered, taking him a willing prisoner. With tender care, he lay down beside Jessica, then suddenly pivoted over her. He feathered his fingers through her hair, brushing it away from her face. Her eyes were huge with wonder. With loving.

"I love you, Jessi."

The words flew like a flaming arrow straight to her heart, yet she was sure she hadn't heard him. Eyes widening, she looked at him. She'd stopped breathing, and in a moment was gasping for air because her lungs were so depleted.

Maybe she was just being delirious. "What did you just say?"

The words had come out without thought, without preamble. But he knew he was bound to them and that he'd meant them. Maybe always meant them. "I said 'I love you,'" he repeated.

It wasn't a forever love, it was a momentary love, an *I love you* born of the moment, destined to die in the next. She knew that. Wouldn't fool herself into thinking anything else. But she'd heard it. Heard it twice and knew that it was more than others had heard in her place. For now it was enough.

Because she didn't want him bound by words that would fade, she kept her own proclamation deep within her, though the words raged to be freed. "I love you," throbbed in her head each time she swallowed it back.

She didn't echo the phrase, didn't say anything. Logan knew he deserved it. Deserved this feeling of being adrift. Of being the one who loved more. Or at all.

Knowing he deserved it still didn't assuage the pain of wanting it. The tenderness burned in the heat of the passion that came after. He slanted his mouth over hers, trying to cleanse himself, to lose himself.

Jessica squirmed, unable to hold back the burst of happiness that sent her spiraling upward to crescents of pleasure. She felt his knee coaxing her legs apart. She opened for him, taking him in and joining him on the ascent to a place she pretended was theirs alone.

I love you, her mind screamed as they reached the final burst of ecstasy.

He'd missed.

He had been so damn close and yet, he'd missed. Missed because he'd heard someone coming. A paunchy, washed-out-looking, gray-garbed guard who would have been sure to have picked him out of a lineup if the man had gotten close enough to see him.

So the shots had been misspent, his goal hadn't been reached, and he'd had to flee.

But now he was through toying. Through waiting. He meant to have his revenge, and he meant to have it soon.

Very, very soon.

Chapter 14

Logan glanced toward his fax machine as he walked into his office behind Jessica. Several pages were piled up in front of the machine on the desk. Jessica's desk. He had to admit he liked the sound of that. Liked having her there beside him. Liked the feel of having her back in his life again.

This time the fit was perfect.

It had been before, he thought. But he hadn't been man enough to admit it then.

He watched Jessica head straight for the desk. "Looks like Albert's been busy again."

Jessica slung her purse strap over the back of her chair. She hadn't thought there was this much left that Albert hadn't already forwarded to her. "He has an extraordinary intimate relationship with the computer. I don't know where I'd be without him."

Curious, feeling the prick of anticipation, Jessica picked up the sheets that had, according to the date she noted stamped across the top, come in around midnight last night.

Just as he was making love with her again, she recalled. A smile curved her mouth as her mind drifted for just a moment. She'd given up trying to block the emotions that overtook her each time she was near Logan, each time she thought of him. She knew what being alone was all about. Knew what aching so bad that it hurt worse than dying was like. That was all ahead of her again. Eyes wide-open, she meant to enjoy what was immediately in front of her before it was gone.

Logan's curiosity was aroused. "Find anything useful?"

She was scanning each page quickly. "Not so far. Hey, wait a minute. *Wait a minute,*" she repeated with more force as the words on the page and their significance registered. Excitedly she began paging faster.

"I'm waiting, I'm waiting," he teased, humoring her. Coming up behind her, he rested his hands on the arms of her chair and leaned over her shoulder. Logan read the slightly blurred letters on the page she was holding. "That's Bart Jenkins's financial statements. I thought you said he was clean."

She had, but obviously she'd been laboring under a misimpression. Her pulse accelerated as pieces started to fall together.

"Not according to this." She glanced at Logan before continuing to read. This *had* to be it. "I didn't know your Mr. Jenkins had Swiss accounts to close out." She spread out several sheets on the desk, comparing them. "By the looks of these statements, he's withdrawing money at a very fast rate."

With the tip of her finger, Jessica followed one month's transactions. "Faster than the money's coming in." She shuffled the pages, looking for the final one. Finding it, she scanned it quickly. Bingo. "You ask me, Mr. Jenkins is a man on the cusp of experiencing a serious cash flow problem if he keeps this up." Jessica drew the pages together into a pile again. "The money can't be going on women because Jenkins doesn't seem to lean in that direction."

Logan grinned at her delicate euphemism. Gripping the armrest, he spun her around so that her chair faced him. "You have been thorough."

"I've a reputation to maintain, remember?"

Growing progressively more excited that this was the lead they'd been looking for, she turned away from Logan and thumbed through the pages all over again. It was all here, the paper trail they needed to confront Jenkins. At least it was a start.

With any luck, it was a finish as well.

Jessica looked at the sums that had gone out and whistled.

"Looks like Mr. Bartholomew Jenkins loves to gamble. These checks are large enough to make my mother blush." Jessica held the page up for Logan to see, pointing at a particularly huge sum.

"And we all know she's no piker." He took the

pages from Jessica and looked them over himself. The accounts were being depleted. There was no doubt about it. Jenkins was in a financial crisis.

Jessica reached for the papers he was holding. "I think I'd like to pay Mr. Jenkins a visit."

He gave them back to her. "Not without me," Logan warned her.

She heard the protective note in his voice. Torn between bristling at the chauvinistic sound of it and being warmed by it, she settled for being diplomatic. "I'm your bodyguard, Logan, not the other way around."

There was no way, for Logan, that she was going to talk him out of going with her no matter what kind of logic she resorted to to convince him. "If it is Jenkins, I'd like my chance at him before we call in the police." When he thought of how the man almost shot Jessica, the world was enveloped in white heat.

She'd never known him to sound that physical before. He'd always been aloof from these kinds of confrontations. He fought with his tongue, his wit, not his fists. This was a side of him that she'd never seen. In a barbaric sort of way, she had to admit it was exciting.

Still, exciting or not, there were rules to follow. "I can't let you slam him around, Logan, no matter how much we'd both like to pummel him if he turns out to be our man."

There was no danger of him taking out his aggressions on Jenkins. If he so much as pushed Jenkins, the man would probably break in half.

"You've obviously never seen Jenkins. The man is a walking toothpick." Though he had to admit that the idea of putting his hands around the man's throat and just shaking him for putting them through this had its appeal. "Let's just say I'd like to have a few words with him before all this goes public."

"We'll see." She held up her hand as he started for the door. "Give me a minute to call Albert. Maybe there's more."

Impatient now that they had something to go on, Logan nodded. He shoved his hands into his pockets, waiting until she made the call.

Jessica had no sooner pressed the last digit of her office telephone number than she heard the receiver on the other end being picked up. "Albert?"

A loud huff of air preceded his stinging greeting. "Where the hell have you been?" he demanded.

She never reacted well to being hauled out on the carpet. Even by someone she cared about. "Where I'm supposed to be. Guarding Logan." She slipped the pages into her purse. "Why didn't you call me about Jerkins's Swiss accounts?"

"I did," Albert countered indignantly. "Several times. Your cell phone insisted you were out of range."

Jessica realized that she'd let the battery run down because of her preoccupation with Logan. She'd let a lot of things go because of Logan.

"And no one seems to want to answer His Majesty's telephone," Albert continued. "I wound up talking to his answering machine."

Looking over her shoulder, Jessica covered the mouthpiece. "Did you check your answering machine this morning?"

Messages had been the last thing on his mind this morning. Waking to find her in his bed, just like old times, he'd taken advantage of the opportunity. Talking to someone from the office hadn't even appeared on his list of priorities.

"No, should I have?"

She just shook her head. "Never mind." Jessica uncovered the receiver. "I'm sorry, Albert, I got caught up in things." She ignored the mumbled, "I'll bet," and continued. "Albert, I just went over the pages you faxed. This is an enormous find on your part. It might be our first break—and none too soon. There was another attempt on Logan's life last night."

A beat passed before she heard from Albert again. "Judging by your calm voice I take it that the attempt fell flat."

She could have sworn he sounded disappointed. She could just hear him after the case was over and Logan faded from her life. Albert would probably spring for a skywriter to write "I told you so" across the sky in huge letters.

"Our record for never losing a client still stands," she assured him. "How did you miss these accounts the first time?"

"Simple. They're under his father's name—seems dear old Bart has power of attorney since his father's mind went south." Sarcasm dripped from Albert's voice. She heard the rustle of papers on the other end. What was he looking for? "One more thing you might want to know. He has a permit for a gun. I checked it against the lab report on those bullets fired at you and golden boy outside the nightclub. Same caliber."

"Better and better," she murmured, jotting down notes to herself on the bottom of the blotter. "You're a gem, Albert."

"So they say." It was his due and he took it as such. "Listen, I need to take the rest of the day off." It wasn't a request, it was a piece of information being tendered.

Albert had never asked for time off. He was completely dedicated to manning his desk. "Albert, are you all right?"

He sighed, surrendering. "If you must know, there's a computer expo being held at the L.A. Convention Center this weekend. We could use a few updates on the equipment," he added defensively.

She wasn't about to keep him from his beloved hobby, especially not after it had helped yield all this information. "Anything you want, Albert."

"My, you sound happy. Logan?"

She wasn't about to go into details, especially not with Albert, not with the way he felt about Logan. "Just glad the case is finally coming together."

"Uh-huh," he said skeptically. "Look, you need to stop by the office. I have the lease sitting on your desk. You need to sign it and get it into the mail today, or come the first of the month we'll find ourselves doing business on the street corner.''

"I'll stop by," she promised.

"See you on Monday, then."

Monday. One way or another, the case would be over. And probably, so would everything else. "Count on it. And have a good time."

"I intend to."

Jessica hung up the receiver.

In Logan's estimation he'd been patient long enough. "So?"

She rose, picking up her purse again, Albert's faxed pages protruding from the top. "Let's go pay Mr. Jenkins a call."

Logan was at the door before she finished her sentence. "Sounds good to me."

The moment they were admitted by the housekeeper and led to the living room and Jenkins, Jessica knew that he was responsible for the threats Logan had been receiving. He didn't even try to act as if he wasn't upset to see them there.

But for the sake of argument, Jessica played it out slowly. After introducing herself, she shook the damp hand that had been half-heartedly extended to her.

Eyes the color of burnt shoe polish moved nervously looking back and forth from Jessica to Logan, Bart Jenkins sat on the edge of the sofa. His hands were busily rubbing out what remained of the creases in his coal gray slacks. He looked ready to jump out of his skin, she thought, taking a seat opposite him and beside Logan on the love seat. The scent of onions unaccountably disturbed her nose and nudged at a memory she couldn't pin down. "Thank you for seeing us, Mr. Jenkins."

Jenkins moved so perilously close to the edge of the sofa, he was in danger of falling off. "I've only a few minutes to spare, you understand." He looked at his watch for emphasis. "I've got an important appointment I can't afford to neglect—before the stockholders meeting," he added as an afterthought. He licked his lips nervously. His shirt was growing damp.

Jessica looked at him pointedly. A bug squirming beneath a microscope. "Would that 'important meeting' have something to do with your gambling debts?"

His complexion, already pale, lost all semblance of color at the bluntly put question.

"What makes you say that?" The question came out in a whisper.

"Common knowledge," she lied, answering before Logan could. She recalled some of the clubs on the statements Albert had faxed her. "Everyone knows that you like to gamble, Mr. Jenkins. That your marker is eagerly accepted in every gambling establishment in Las Vegas—and parts closer. You haven't had a lucky day in months."

The markers that were making him sweat weren't the ones held by reputable casinos, but by a far darker element residing in the gambling world. Men who weren't afraid to take their payment out in trade if all else failed.

Logan leaned closer. "Where's all the money coming from, Jenkins?"

Hostility flared in the dark eyes. Jenkins glared at him. "Not that it's any business of yours, but I have a great many assets." The expression on Logan's face made him squirm.

The next question only intensified Jenkins's reaction. "Does your father know you're siphoning off his accounts, Bart?"

Beads of perspiration broke out in a thin, watery line along his upper lip. Jenkins pressed them together, running a nervous hand through hair that had begun to thin out prematurely several years ago.

"My father's not a well man right now. He can't be troubled about these things."

Onions. Now she remembered. She'd caught a strong scent of onions when she'd entered the alley opposite The In Place. Jenkins had been in the alley, sweating profusely.

Incensed, Jessica attacked him from the other side. "Where's your gun, Bart?"

He jumped as if he'd forgotten she was there. Like a cornered rodent, he lashed out in fear. "I don't have a gun."

Jenkins looked far too nervous to be a cold-blooded killer. But men who had their backs pushed against the wall did desperate things. She watched him for any sudden moves.

"According to the registration report, you do. The same kind of gun that was used to shoot at Logan."

"You're crazy." The denial exploded in a sudden volley.

"Are we?" Logan asked calmly. "Then let us have the gun, Bart. We can have a few simple tests run and clear all this up for you right away."

Trapped and frightened, Jenkins didn't know which way to turn, what to say or think. It wasn't supposed to have gone this way. Logan was supposed to back down, thinking that opposing the merger wasn't worth the risk of having something happen to him. Instead, now he was the one at risk. "I—I—"

Getting up, Jessica crossed to the telephone and picked up the receiver. "If you don't want to be co-operative, I'll have to call the police and—"

As if propelled by a hidden force, Jenkins bolted across the room to her. Logan was on his feet instantly, but all Jenkins did was slam his hand down on the receiver, breaking any connection.

"No, don't please. I just meant to frighten him." Frantically he looked at Logan, appealing to him. To his sense of fair play. "Honest, Logan. I just wanted to frighten you, nothing else." His lips twisted in an envious, pathetic grimace that passed for a smile. "You could talk a river out of flowing, and I *needed* this deal to go through."

Jessica undid the second and third buttons on Logan's shirt, moving back the material to expose the thick bandage. "Enough to try to kill him?"

Jenkins shook his head so hard, it seemed not to

be connected to his neck. "I didn't try to kill him." And then the sight of the bandage registered. His eyes widened. "Omigod, did I do that?"

Rebuttoning his shirt, Logan looked at Jenkins incredulously. "You didn't even know?"

"No, I swear. I just fired over your heads. I thought… Oh, God, I've made such a mess of everything." Covering his face, Jenkins sank down on the sofa again. A wasted shell of a man. "And now I'm going to prison." The words were followed by a barely stifled sob.

Logan's anger slipped away. There seemed to be no point to it. Jenkins probably didn't even know what he was doing. And the man had enough demons to deal with already. "You're not going to prison, Bart." Out of the corner of his eye, he saw Jessica staring at him.

"What are you saying, Logan? He shot you."

Logan believed Jenkins when he'd said he hadn't meant to. "Look at him, Jessi." He gestured toward Jenkins. "The man's a pathetic screwup, but he's not a murderer. Just being faced with having to pay back his debts should be punishment enough for him." More than enough, Logan added silently. "It wasn't as if he was actually trying to kill me."

"I wasn't, I wasn't," Jenkins bleated.

"There, you see. He wasn't."

In Jessica's eyes Logan was treating this far too lightly. "Whether or not he 'actually' meant to, he could have. You'd be just as dead if he aimed for you, or accidentally miscalculated."

And she cared, he thought. Whether he lived or died, she cared. The rest didn't matter as much as he'd thought. "Jessi, you were supposed to find out who was sending the threatening letters. You found him. Case closed."

"You have to call the police, Logan," she insisted. "He threatened to bomb one of your buildings."

Logan sincerely doubted that Jenkins had meant to carry out that threat.

"I know that every kid can look up how to make a bomb on the Internet these days, but I doubt very much if Jenkins could put it together even with the easiest instructions." He looked over toward the man. "All part of the ploy, right Bart?"

"Right. Oh, God, right." Intensity increased in his voice with each word. "Logan, if you could just find it in your heart—"

Logan cut him off. "Don't beg, Jenkins. It'll just turn my stomach. Just put your house in order," Logan advised.

Jessica couldn't believe what she was hearing. She could remember when Logan's competitive spirit escalated until he was ready to decimate everyone in his path on the track. She'd always assumed that that killer instinct carried over to all parts of his life. It was a revelation to learn it hadn't.

"Then you're just going to walk away from him?"

"Drawing and quartering's frowned on these days." Logan glanced down at the shoulder she'd just used for show-and-tell. "Besides, my shoulder's mending. No harm done."

But it could have been. It could have been. Jessica shook her head. The decision ultimately was Logan's. "If you say so." She looked at Jenkins. "Count yourself lucky."

"Oh, I am, I am." Like a puppet being jerked to its feet, he sprang up. "You have my full support, Logan, no matter what you want to do with the company. My absolute full support."

Logan doubted it.... Not that it mattered. Jenkins's neck was on the line. He would still try to get people to change their minds. But he lacked the persuasive powers to sway anyone.

Logan stood for a moment, looking at Jenkins. He hated to see anyone twisting in the wind this way.

"Call my lawyer after the meeting, Bart. I'll arrange some kind of loan for you—as long as you sign a statement to get help with that gambling problem of yours."

Jenkins stared at him as if Logan had just walked across water. He grasped his hand. "I don't know what to say. You're a saint, Logan. A saint."

"Yeah, right," Logan said under his breath. He slipped his hand along Jessica's waist. "Let's go, Jess. I've got things to do."

"You are, you know," she said to him as they walked out. "An utter saint. I don't know anyone else who'd have done that for a man who'd made him feel as if he were being stalked."

But Logan dismissed the act of charity. "Let's just say I've got a few good deeds to catch up on."

"Speaking of catching up, I'll catch up with you later."

He didn't understand. "Why?"

"I need to get down to the office. I've got a lease to sign and get in the mail."

Logan frowned. "Can't it wait? The meeting's in an hour."

The case was closed. For all intents and purposes, their association was over. She wanted to make the break before he did. "You don't need me anymore. We just got our confession."

Logan blew out a breath. Well, that hadn't gone well. "What if he's not working alone?"

She didn't bother stifling her laugh. "You really think that's a conspirator in there?"

No, he didn't, and he knew that matter was settled. But not the matter between them. He needed time.

"Humor me," he urged.

She thought of the lease. "All right." Jessica did a few quick calculations, taking travel to her office and then to his into account. "I can be there in less than an hour."

Logan had a monkey wrench to throw into the gears. "But I have to stop at the office." Though he was good on his feet, he wanted the notes he'd left on his desk, just in case.

"No problem. I'll meet you there." She saw the doubt entering his eyes. Did having her along matter that much to him? Something inside her warmed, though she warned herself not to get carried away.

She'd already learned the danger in that. "I promise."

He'd have to settle on that. "I'll hold you to it."

Dropping Logan off at the Buchanan building, Jessica went on to her own office. A bittersweet feeling traveled with her. The same one that always came after a case was wrapped up. But this time it was accentuated because it was not only the end of the case, but of their being together.

Oh, what they had between them might linger a week or so more. A month at the outside, but she knew Logan. He liked to move on.

She'd learned that the hard way.

"No use crying over what can't be," she murmured to herself, unlocking the door to her office.

"What would you cry over?"

The question was accompanied by the press of gun barrel to her temple.

"It's about time you showed up. I've been waiting for you."

The office door slammed shut behind her, underscoring the malevolent words.

Chapter 15

Jessica tried to move her head back. The sound of the hammer being cocked had her freezing instantly. "What do you want?"

The rumbling sound of the mirthless laugh drove steel spikes through her.

"Still haven't figured it out? And here I thought you were so clever. Just goes to show your reputation is really overstated." Still standing behind her, the man brought his mouth next to her ear. "I want you to suffer, of course. Really suffer."

Jessica drew on the philosophy she'd fashioned that had seen her through life as well as her career: courage with common sense. Careful not to make a sudden move, she pulled her head back as far as she was safely able, to look at him. This time he let her.

Recognition was instant. "You're the telephone repairman."

Dressed in brown slacks and a beige shirt, all suited to making him blend in anywhere, the man inclined his head in a mocking bow.

"Guilty as charged." The malevolent smile on his lips faded, replaced by one that made her blood run cold. "Guilty as charged," he repeated, his voice cold, hard. "Doesn't ring any bells? How about Rex Wallace? That do it for you?" he demanded.

Rex Wallace.

Her first case.

That was where she knew him from. He reminded her of Wallace. Except that he was much too young. Wallace had been in his late fifties. Desperate, Jessica tried to fit the man in her office into the past.

The case had involved insurance fraud. Rex Wallace had initially hired her for his company, thinking that by bringing her in, he could control the investigation. He'd almost managed to get away with it, if it hadn't been for a lucky break on her part.

The resemblance was not in his face, but in the attitude his body exuded. The arrogant set of his shoulders nudged at memories.

"Are you his son?"

"Very good. Baxter," he introduced himself magnanimously.

His eyes on hers, Wallace slowly slid the tip of the steel barrel down along her throat. Pleasure bubbled through his veins as he watched the pulse there jump.

He wanted her afraid. Very afraid. The way his father had been.

Her fingernails digging into her palms, Jessica forced herself not to flinch. She had to think, to try to reason with him.

"Your father made a mistake, Wallace. There's no reason for you to make one, too."

The laugh was short, dismissive. "I already did when I shot your boyfriend instead of you."

She looked at him in disbelief. "That was you? But—" And then she realized that Jenkins had only mistakenly thought he'd shot Logan. He'd been the shooter outside the nightclub. It was Wallace who had been waiting for them outside the banquet hall last night.

Two, there had been two, she upbraided herself. Two men with different agendas. No wonder it had been so confusing.

"That was me. But this time it's close range and I won't miss."

She thought her heart would stop as he ran the barrel down her chest. There was no leverage for her to use, no space to turn to her advantage. All he had to do was squeeze the trigger and it would be over.

Jessica tried to keep him talking, searching for a way to distract Wallace. "Why do you want to kill me?"

Contempt twisted his mouth. "Because of you, my father's dead."

He saw the confusion in her eyes, and the temptation to shoot was almost overwhelming. At the last moment he managed to restrain the impulse.

Not until he'd carried out his plan, he promised himself.

"My father hung himself in prison last month, unable to take the shame any longer. And now I'm going to make you pay for it." His eyes were as cold as winter steel. "I'm through toying with you."

The pieces were all jumbled in her mind. She tried to arrange them, to separate Jenkins from Wallace. "You sent the roses?"

He wondered when she'd figure that out. "Very good. I wanted you to feel scared, unsure. Like my father was in prison all that time." Breathing hard, the momentum built in his voice. "He didn't belong there. He was a decent man who made a mistake. You broke him," Wallace shouted into her face.

"Decent men don't defraud the company they're working for of over a million dollars and then try to pin the blame on someone else," she pointed out. Jessica saw the red color flare into his face.

"It's a damn insurance company!" he sputtered. "It defrauds people everyday!"

Hysteria was mounting in his voice, in his face. Any second he would be pulling the trigger. Desperate, she tried to divert his agitation.

"How did you know where I was?" She would have known, she thought, if he'd been tailing her.

The moment the question was out of her mouth, the answer came to her. She looked at the telephone. Of course. It was so simple, it never occurred to her.

She'd called Albert, apprising him of her every move. "You bugged the office phone, didn't you?"

"Right again." Training the gun on her, he stepped back, giving her clear access to the telephone. He pointed at it. "Call him."

She didn't understand. "What?"

Explaining things was beginning to irritate him. "Call your boyfriend."

For a second time, everything within her froze. "Why?"

"Because I want to kill him," Wallace growled. And then he smiled. Jessica wasn't sure which was worse. "And I want you to watch."

"No."

Incensed, Wallace waved the gun, aiming it at her head. There was no question in her mind that he'd shoot without compunction if she refused him a second time. If she were dead she couldn't help Logan, and Jessica had a gut feeling that Wallace wouldn't stop with just killing her. He'd kill Logan, too. Somehow, in his twisted mind, that would even the score.

She exhaled the breath she'd been holding slowly. "All right."

Pleased, he could afford to be generous. "That a girl."

Jessica's fingertips felt slippery as she pressed the numbers to Logan's office on the keypad. Each time the telephone rang on the other end, the sound reverberated in her head, adding depth and breadth to her headache.

When Logan finally picked up the telephone, she

thought she'd lost all the air in her lungs. With effort she forced herself to sound calm.

"Logan, could you come down to my office, please? I have something to show you."

Wallace's smile widened at what he saw as irony in her entreaty.

"Jessi, you know there's no time." Logan sounded bewildered at her request. "I—"

Jessica cut in before he could finish. "Don't argue with me," she said sweetly. "If you're going to be this stubborn about a simple request, then I just might call off our wedding."

"Wedding?" Logan echoed.

Please, please, please *understand, Logan.* "Uh-huh. Right. Good. That's what I said," she said in reply to nothing. "Come right over. I'll be waiting."

Wallace pushed down on the cradle, breaking the connection before she had the opportunity to add anything. "Congratulations on your engagement. Too bad you won't be around to make the ceremony. But the good news is, neither will the groom."

No matter what happened to her, she couldn't let him hurt Logan. "Wallace, it's not too late to give this up."

"Oh, but it is. Way too late." His expression was bitter. "It's too late for my father, so it's too late for you and your boyfriend. Now sit down over there where I can watch you while we wait for your boyfriend to come to his execution."

Jessica felt sick. What if she didn't come up with anything? What if—

She had to get Wallace to change his mind. "Why drag him into this? Your grudge is with me."

"That's exactly why I'm 'dragging him into this.' Because he means something to you. And I want you to feel pain before you die, bitch. I want your heart to feel like it's been ripped out by its roots the way my mother did when they took my father away."

"Your mother?" She seized the bit of information. "What would she say if she knew you were doing this?"

"Leave her out of this," he ordered malevolently. "Now sit down!"

Jessica did as she was told, her mind working frantically.

When she heard the knock on her door twenty minutes later, Jessica nearly jumped out of her skin. All attempts at reasoning with Wallace had only gotten him more agitated. Like a hair trigger, he was set to go off at any moment, at the slightest provocation.

She shouldn't have called Logan. Her time was up and nothing had changed. She hadn't managed to get the drop on Wallace. Her one attempt had ended up earning her a pistol-whipping across her face. She could feel a welt beginning to rise.

Her one hope was that Logan had come prepared.

Wallace motioned her to her feet. She looked longingly toward her purse, and the pistol that was in it, but Wallace had kicked it across the room when she'd entered.

"Jessi, it's me," Logan called to her. "Open the door."

Wallace cocked his gun. "Go ahead," he mouthed.

It was going to take timing, she thought. Afraid that Wallace would fire the moment she opened the door, she psyched herself up to push Logan to the ground the instant she saw him.

Instead, as she turned the knob and opened the door, Jessica found herself being grabbed by the arm and yanked off to the side.

"Get down, Jessi!" Logan shouted at her just before she heard two shots ring out.

Or maybe both shots came at the same time.

Recovering, she spun around to see Logan holding a gun. Wallace was on the floor, clutching his knee, his own gun out of reach.

Logan could only spare her a quick glance. Even so, he saw the welt and the discoloration on her cheek. Rage gripped his belly. The temptation to kill the man on the floor was overwhelming.

Instead, Logan moved toward her, his eyes never leaving the vermin on the floor. "Are you all right, Jessi?"

Jessica was beside him immediately, drawing air into her shaky lungs. She didn't want to dwell on what might have happened just now. Didn't want to think about it at all.

"I'm okay."

Moving quickly, she picked up the gun that Wallace had dropped, keeping well out of range. Cursing at them vehemently, he pressed his hands against his knee. Blood oozed through his fingers. Backing up, Jessica looked at the gun Logan was holding trained on Wallace.

"Where did you—"

He anticipated her question. "Borrowed," was all he said. No need to tell her that he'd gotten the gun for protection a long time ago. He knew how her mind worked. "Nice bit of double talk on the phone earlier. For a second I thought I'd slipped into a parallel universe." One where things had actually worked out for them. Logan saw her reaching for the telephone receiver. He knew she was going to call the police. "Don't bother, the police are on their way."

She replaced the receiver and could only shake her head in amazement. "God, but you are efficient."

"I've learned." The air was turning a bright blue courtesy of Wallace's mouth. Logan went on talking as if Wallace wasn't in the room. "Who is he?"

Someone who almost killed you. Because of me. She dragged a hand through her hair and realized that it was shaking. She dropped it to her side.

"The son of someone who was sent to jail on evidence I uncovered." She had no time to say anything else. The police began arriving.

She recognized Detective Kane Madigan from previous dealings she'd had. Relieved at having to deal with a familiar face, she filled him in as quickly as she could. There was little for Logan to add.

He glanced at his watch. Time was growing incredibly short. He took Jessica's hand. "C'mon, I still have to make that meeting."

Kane closed his small notebook, stuffing it into the back pocket of his jeans. "We're going to need you at the station for a formal statement."

Logan nodded. "As soon as this meeting is over," he promised. "But I really need to be there."

Kane understood. He wasn't unfamiliar with the Buchanan name. A half smile cracked his serious expression. "Need an escort?"

It would be a relief not to have to drive to the meeting with one eye on his rearview mirror. "Brother, do we."

"Let's go, then." With one hand to each of their backs, Kane escorted them out of the office, leaving Wallace to his patrolmen.

The stockholders meeting was already in progress by the time they'd arrived. Holding her hand in his—"for luck," he'd told her—Logan rushed into the company's auditorium and up toward the stage.

Jessica noted that Dane actually looked relieved when they walked in. His concern for his brother obviously transcended any differences in policy or opinion that they had.

And to think she'd suspected him. And hadn't a clue about Wallace. So much for gut instincts, she mused, taking a seat near the front.

Sitting back, Jessica watched Logan take the podium. And in short order, take his audience as well. His impassioned speech about traditions and loyalties needing to be placed in the foreground again rather than outweighed by possible financial compensations struck a chord with the crowd. Sporadic applause was sprinkled liberally throughout his speech, underscoring key points.

He was a natural-born speaker. A natural-born leader. He'd wasted a lot of years, but this was where he belonged, she thought. And she was proud of him.

She was going to miss him.

Riding high on the success of the vote that had just been taken, Logan jumped from the stage, looking for Jessica. He needed her with him to share this moment.

But the seat he'd seen her take was empty now. Looking around, he didn't see her. A little of his high slipped away.

The throng tightened around him, all well-wishers congratulating him on his speech, his sentiment, his victory. The words buzzed around his ears as he searched for Jessica. Shaking hands, murmuring appropriate responses, Logan worked his way through the crowd.

He finally found her near the door of the auditorium. She was leaving.

In a sudden flash, he saw his life leaving, as well.

"Jessi, wait up."

Jessica stopped. She'd hoped to make the break clean. To leave while he was still busy. Forcing herself to look cheerful, she turned around.

"I was just going to the police station to give Detective Madigan my statement."

No, she wasn't, he thought. She was leaving. Really leaving. He took her hand, going along with the lie. "We'll go together."

She slipped her hand from his and took a step back. Edging away from him. "I thought you'd be busy with them." She nodded toward the stockholders. "You really roused them. Maybe you *should* think about running for political office."

The hell with political office. The hell with everything. Nothing mattered if she walked out now. "Jessi, what's wrong?"

She shrugged off the concern she saw in his eyes and forced her voice to sound disinterested.

"Nothing's wrong. The case is over—as well as the complications," she recited. "With Wallace in custody and Jenkins contrite, as well as forever in your debt, there's no reason for me to stick around."

His eyes pinned her. Did she really mean that? Had he lost her again? Or was she just trying to pay him back? "None?"

She didn't want to talk anymore. If she didn't go now, she might never have the strength to go at all. And she had to go, go before he ripped her heart out a second time. Not willfully, not with malice—but he would.

"The bill'll be in the mail," she replied, turning away.

She'd only managed to take two steps toward the doorway before she heard him.

"I'm sorry."

Certain that she was imagining it, Jessica turned

around and looked at him. Inside she was trembling, though she called herself a fool. "What?"

"I'm sorry," he repeated, louder this time and with more feeling.

He didn't care who heard him. Logan cut the distance between them. At least physically. The rest, only she could do.

"I'm sorry I hurt you, sorry I ever let you out of my life." Once started, he just kept going. "Sorry I was so afraid of my feelings, but I was. I'd always been able to call the shots before, Jess. Always been able to walk away when the spirit moved me. But that time, with you, I couldn't. That look in your eyes, that sweet, innocent look, held me like nothing else ever had before. I had no control anymore. My feelings were controlling me. Scaring the hell out of me.

"I guess what I was most afraid of was not just that I had no control, but that one day you'd walk away and leave me."

"So you left instead?" she asked incredulously. How did that possibly make any sense?

"Yeah, I left instead." He realized how stupid that had to sound to her. Because it *had* been stupid. He knew that now. "But alone is alone, Jessi, and it didn't matter how I got there. I didn't gain anything by trying to outsmart my feelings. I lost everything. And I will again if you walk out of my life." He took her hands in his, a silent entreaty in his eyes. "I love you, Jessi. I always have. I always will. I'm just not afraid to say it anymore. Not afraid to feel it."

He took a breath, trying to deal with all the raw

emotions that were coursing through his veins. All the raw emotions that had been stirred up in the last few hours.

"When you called me and I heard that tightness in your voice, I knew you were in trouble. You didn't have to say anything more. And I was scared, scared that something would happen to you before I could get there. I've never been so scared in my life."

"Even more than when you were on the track?"

"That was a piece of cake in comparison." He opened his heart up completely to her. "You mean everything to me, Jessi, and I don't want to lose you again. I couldn't live through it." His eyes searched hers, looking for an indication that she understood. More, that she felt the same as he did. "What do I have to do to make you stay? I swear I'll do anything you want."

They'd come a long way this past week. A long way. She'd seen him in a completely different light, as not just the master of his own fate, but a generous man who'd taken on a huge responsibility and shouldered it well. She'd grown herself. No longer the hopelessly in love woman she'd been, she was now a match for him. And just as in love as she'd ever been.

Jessica smiled at him. "You just did it. All I ever wanted was for you to love me—for you to admit you loved me," she amended.

Was it that easy? Really that easy? "I'll do more than admit it. I'll take out a two-page ad in the *Sunday Times* for everyone to read."

Humor curved her mouth. "Just a two-page ad?"

"Bigger. I'll buy out the whole damn paper if you want." He drew her into his arms. Where she belonged. "But for right now, would you settle for having me say it in front of the minister?"

She turned her face up to his. "I don't see that as settling at all."

As he brought his mouth down to hers to seal their future, Logan knew he was finally running toward happiness and not away from it.

* * * * *

∇INTIMATE MOMENTS®

™ *Silhouette*®

and

DOREEN ROBERTS

invite you to the wonderful world of

RODEO MEN

A secret father, a passionate protector,
a make-believe groom—these cowboys are
husbands waiting to happen....

HOME IS WHERE THE COWBOY IS
IM #909, February 1999

A FOREVER KIND OF COWBOY
IM #927, May 1999

THE MAVERICK'S BRIDE
IM #945, August 1999

Don't miss a single one!

Available at your favorite retail outlet.

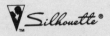

™

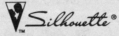

#925 CATTLEMAN'S PROMISE—Marilyn Pappano
Heartbreak Canyon

Guthrie Harris was shocked when Olivia Miles and her twin daughters showed up on his Oklahoma ranch—with a deed!—and claimed it was *their* home. But since they had nowhere else to go, the longtime loner let them stay. And the longer Olivia stuck around, the less Guthrie wanted her to leave—his home *or* his heart.

#926 CLAY YEAGER'S REDEMPTION—Justine Davis
Trinity Street West

Clay Yeager hadn't meant to trespass on Casey Scott's property—but he was glad he had. The emotions this ex-cop had kept buried for so long were back in full force. Then Casey became a stranger's target, and Clay knew the time had come to protect his woman. He was done with moving on—he was ready to move in!

#927 A FOREVER KIND OF COWBOY—Doreen Roberts
Rodeo Men

Runaway heiress Lori Ashford had little experience when it came to men. So when she fell for rugged rodeo rider Cord McVane, what she felt was something she'd never known existed. But would the brooding cowboy ever see that the night she'd discovered passion in his arms was just the beginning—of forever?

#928 THE TOUGH GUY AND THE TODDLER—Diane Pershing
Men in Blue

Detective Dominic D'Annunzio thought nothing could penetrate his hardened heart—until beautiful but haunted Jordan Carlisle needed his assistance. But Jordan wasn't just looking for help, she was looking for miracles. And the closer they came to the truth, the more Dom began wondering what was in charge of this case—his head or his heart?

#929 HER SECOND CHANCE FAMILY—Christine Scott
Families Are Forever

Maggie Conrad and her son were finally on their own—*and* on the run. But the small town of Wyndchester offered the perfect hideaway. Then the new sheriff, Jason Gallagher, moved in next door, and Maggie feared her secret wouldn't stay that way for long. Could Maggie keep her past hidden while learning that love *was* better the second time around?

#930 KNIGHT IN A WHITE STETSON—Claire King
Way Out West

Calla Bishop was desperate to save her family's ranch. And as the soon-to-be-wife of a wealthy businessman, she was about to secure her birthright. Then she hired Henry Beckett, and it wasn't long before this wrangler had roped himself one feisty cowgirl. But would Henry's well-kept secret cause Calla to hand over her beloved ranch—and her guarded heart?